Their eyes met and held, and he was close enough that she could feel his body heat, even against the competing heat of the scorching air.

He cupped a hand ⟨...⟩ aist, leaned toward ⟨...⟩ ear, 'Strange, isn't ⟨...⟩ eld again, just the wa⟨...⟩

'Oh.' Her brain ⟨...⟩ her body in its reaction to his nearness. She was shocked at how familiar he was to her senses after so long. 'What do you mean, a level playing field?'

'We're both highly competent in certain areas, with plenty of crisis situations under our belts, but we know nothing about an emergency of this particular kind.' His mouth hardly moved; this was for her alone. 'We're going to be stretched to breaking point tonight, the way we were sometimes during our internship.'

Her eyes were still locked with his. Narrowed as they were in the harsh light, she could see the evidence of the years that had passed. He had faint lines there now. The kind you wanted to kiss…

She was astonished that she still felt this pull towards him.

'If it helps,' he added, 'I'm very glad that you're here.'

Lilian Darcy is Australian, but has strong ties to the USA through her American husband. They have four growing children, and currently live in Canberra, Australia. Lilian has written over fifty romance novels, and still has more story ideas crowding into her head than she knows what to do with. Her work has appeared on romance bestsellers list, and two of her plays have been nominated for major Australian writing awards. 'I'll keep writing as long as people keep reading my books,' she says. 'It's all I've ever wanted to do, and I love it.'

THE DOCTOR'S FIRE RESCUE

BY
LILIAN DARCY

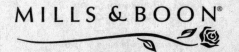

MILLS & BOON®

First published in Great Britain 2005
Harlequin Mills & Boon Limited,
Eton House, 18-24 Paradise Road, Richmond, Surrey TW9 1SR

© Lilian Darcy 2005

ISBN 0 263 84304 1

Set in Times Roman 10½ on 12 pt.
03-0505-50015

Printed and bound in Spain
by Litografia Rosés, S.A., Barcelona

CHAPTER ONE

'ALISON!'

Dr Alison Lane froze at the sound of her name, then relaxed as a half-turn on the swivel chair brought her face to face with Michael Goodwin. He was a local Australian paediatric lung specialist, who'd done a visiting fellowship at her hospital in Ohio a few years ago, and his *wasn't* the voice she'd dreaded to hear, thank goodness!

'Mike!' She stood up from the computer terminal with a smile, hoping he hadn't detected her relief, since she could hardly explain the reason for it. She gave him a quick hug. 'It's good to see you. I saw your name on the programme.'

'Speaking this afternoon, then heading back to Sydney straight away. I just drove up this morning.'

'Oh, I'm disappointed that you're not staying.'

Because she liked Mike, but more because she was looking for camouflage, decoys, plenty of excuses on tap for fleeing an unwanted conversation over the next few days. There was another familiar name she'd seen on the conference programme, not a welcome one. She might need all the avoidance strategies she could come up with.

'Really can't, though.' Mike grinned. 'Charlotte and I have our first baby due on Saturday.'

'Oh, that's wonderful!'

'And she's been asking me these ominous questions about real versus false contractions, as if Obstetrics is something I'm supposed to know about…'

'Which you don't any more, because all you know about is lungs. I'm familiar with that phenomenon!' Alison was a

5

pulmonologist, too, with a particular expertise in infant respiration.

'Tend to dread those occasional announcements on aeroplanes, don't you? "Is there a doctor on board this flight?" Well, yes, but only if the patient is under sixteen and having an asthma attack. Want to grab a coffee?' Mike suggested.

'Yes, please! It'll give me an excuse to stop this.' She gestured at the computer screen, which was showing a difficult-to-navigate website in garish black and yellow.

'What have you been doing in here anyhow?' Mike asked. He eyed the cluster of computers, copiers and fax machines in the conference hotel's business centre. 'I came past and saw that distinctive hair of yours.'

'Trying and failing to find a pulmonology joke on the Internet to start off my presentation tomorrow,' Alison answered.

She made a questioning gesture regarding the computer to the woman behind the business centre's front desk. Do I have to switch this thing off or something?

Apparently not.

'I'm starting mine with a pulmonology joke this afternoon,' Mike said, as they left.

'Oh, you found one? Lucky!'

'Stole it from a colleague. I can pass it on to you, if you want. I'm not wedded to it. Too jittery about Charlotte and the baby.'

'Tell me all about it, Mike.'

'Don't say that unless you mean it. We're thrilled. We'd been trying for a while, so we're capable of boring people on the subject quite severely. We can order coffee right here, if you want,' he interrupted himself. They'd reached an open lounge area in the large hotel lobby. 'Chairs are comfortable.'

'Looks good.' She sat down. 'And I really would like to hear about the baby. Have you—'

The hotel check-in desk appeared in her vision, across half an acre of shiny marble floor, and there he was, standing in front of it.

Niccolo.

Nico, to his friends.

She hadn't seen him in seven years.

'Decided on names yet?' she finished in a tone that sounded woolly and quite different to her own ears. Oh, yes, she'd been right to dread this moment.

Mike didn't pick up on the change.

'Only if it's a boy,' he said. 'Adam James. For a girl, Charlotte has gone all loopy on jewel names. Garnet and Ruby and Topaz. I'm resisting but crumbling fast. She thinks all my ideas are way too plain. Sarah. Susan.'

'I'm sure you'll find the right thing in the end.' Alison didn't know what she was saying. Mike passed the laminated menu to her and she barely remembered what it was for. Coffee? Why had she thought she wanted coffee?

She hadn't known Niccolo Conti would be at this conference until she'd received the finalised programme in the mail a few weeks ago. He wasn't giving a paper. He was here as the representative of his family's huge pharmaceutical corporation, which had recently bought out an almost equally huge manufacturer of high-tech medical equipment.

So he was just a glorified sales rep really, she told herself, then almost laughed at how ludicrous that sounded. She would never be able to think of a man like Niccolo Conti that way, and even if she could it would do nothing to change her feelings about him.

He was leaning over the high desk signing something, while the uniformed blonde behind it didn't trouble to hide her first impression of him—socks knocked off, basically—

because she didn't think anyone was looking. Wow! said her face.

We can form a support group together, Alison thought. Stitch up each other's broken hearts.

'Put on a fair bit of weight,' Mike said.

No, he hadn't. Nico still had the same rugged and un-compromising male physique she'd once known in intimate detail. He was thirty-four years old and at the very apex of his prime. What on earth was Mike talking about?

Charlotte. Of course.

'Is her doctor concerned?' Alison asked, dragging her focus back to where it should have been all along.

'Not really. But he thinks it's going to be a big baby. We've been hoping she'd be a bit early, but the clock's running out on that option.'

'I'm sure everything will be fine. Doctors always worry too much, don't they? I mean, not Charlotte's doctor, but the two of you, because you're both…' Was she making any sense at all?

'Doctors,' Mike agreed. 'I know.'

Niccolo was coming this way, in search of the elevators that led to the upper two floors. They were behind him, in fact. So was the sign on the wall that would have told him this. His frown gave him a forbidding look, in contrast to the killer smile that had done such drastic things to the re-ceptionist's socks half a minute ago.

Alison lifted the menu in front of her face and muttered, 'Now, let me see…' as if choosing a five-course meal at a Michelin three-star restaurant.

She must look ridiculous, and what was the point? Her red-gold hair had already acted as a beacon to Mike. It would do the same for Nico. And if she'd seen his name on the conference programme, he'd surely have seen hers. If he wanted to avoid her, then he would, and if he wanted to seek her out—ha!—then he'd do that with equal facility, and the same understated charm that had always cut right through her defences and her doubts.

'Emotionally literate' was how a mutual friend had described Nico once. It was an inflated phrase, but it was accurate. He'd often seemed to understand her better than she'd understood herself.

'I'm just having a flat white,' Mike said, looking a little startled at Alison's performance with the menu. Niccolo Conti had been long gone from her life by the time she and Mike had worked together in Ohio.

'I was just thinking the same thing,' she answered, and put it down.

Nico wasn't in sight.

How *stupid* to feel disappointed about it!

Seconds later she saw him coming back in the direction he should have been going in all along, towards the elevators. Lifts, as people called them here in Australia. He was still looking for them. He must have jet lag after a long flight from Rome or London or heaven knew where, because she'd never seen him looking lost before.

No.

Once, maybe.

His gaze canvassed the large lobby, arrowed towards the dimly lit bar on the other side, skated past the gift shop just off the entrance, and then fell on the grouped lounge chairs where Alison and Mike sat.

He saw her.

She knew he did. His startling golden-green eyes locked with hers unmistakably, even though there was no acknowledgement in his face at all. He had to recognise her. She hadn't changed very much. She still had the same flag-waving hair, which she kept loose when she wasn't working, as a reminder to herself that this was down-time. Her pale

Scottish-Scandinavian skin was genetic and in place for life, with the blue eyes to match. And even though she'd always considered her neat nose more pointy than dainty, she hadn't gone under the knife to rectify the problem.

But, no, he didn't smile or lift his hand or let his mouth drop open in horror. She thought she detected a tightening of his jaw muscles, but at this distance it was hard to tell. Some normality-seeking impulse led her to raise her hand in a wave despite his lack of reaction, but he probably didn't see because he'd turned now and had spotted the bank of elevators angled back from the far side of the long check-in desk.

At last.

A few seconds later, he'd disappeared.

'So, catch me up on everything that's been happening for you,' Mike said, and she managed to enjoy their coffee together after all.

The thunderstorm began at eight o'clock that night.

Alison had spent the afternoon as a diligent conference attendee at this, the Fourth Annual Pacific Rim Conference on Paediatric Pulmonology, held in the mountain resort village of Corinbye, New South Wales. As a gesture of friendship, she sat in on Mike's presentation straight after lunch, even though his topic wasn't directly relevant to her own current area of specialisation.

He began to look harried halfway through his co-presenter's paper, and she only just managed to grab him on the way out to wish him and Charlotte all the best with the birth. He already had his car keys in his hand.

'Hoping to make it home before dark,' he told her.

The late afternoon session was interesting and well attended, but Alison didn't see Niccolo there. She told herself that she wasn't looking but, oh, she was lying!

He was highly visible at the conference's crowded opening reception, however. Tailored Italian suit in a shade of grey-beige that would have looked too pale on most men. Dark head, with hair cut short. Tall but not towering. She got close enough to him at one point to detect a few threads of silver in the black, and found herself wondering if any particular life trials had put them there.

Her curiosity on the subject rattled and disturbed her. So did the little kick in her heartbeat. After seven years, she shouldn't be remotely interested any more, let alone empathetic. As for the way she dreaded any kind of confrontation, or even a polite, superficial chat, she wasn't a big fan of anything that took her beyond her comfort zone, and Nico would definitely do that.

Following this near encounter with him, she put all her avoidance strategies into operation. She holed up at the bar and stared at the bubbles in her ginger ale. She stalked waiters with their trays of canapés, pretending starvation. She pinned distant professional acquaintances against the wall and shot questions at them about their current research until they got a glazed and panicky look in their eyes and started edging away.

It wasn't funny, really.

Nico must have seen her—*must* have!—but he seemed no more inclined to generate an awkward meeting than she was, and of course he was three times smoother at avoiding one than she could ever hope to be. He'd been schooled in fastidious and aristocratic European etiquette since birth, while her own hard-working single mother in Chicago had barely had the energy left by the end of the day to give reminders about please and thank you. Mother and daughter had both lived rather narrow, joyless lives back then.

After an hour and a half of reception-style schmoozing and smiling while balancing little bits of food in her hand,

Alison had had enough. Back in her room at the far end of the outermost concourse of ground-level guest rooms, she changed into jeans, a purple cropped top and white leather walking shoes, put her hair in a ponytail and went to explore the nature trail she'd read about in a hotel brochure.'

Much better.

Since this was Australia and it was mid-December, the daylight was still strong and bright, even though it was after six-thirty. Approaching the start of the marked walking track, she got some great views of the vacation-oriented alpine village perched on steeply sloping ground above the sprawl of the hotel. The architecture drew on varied influences from Europe and North America as well as colonial Australia, and was quaint and cute and attractive.

There were other people on the nature trail—families and couples—so she felt perfectly safe even when she thought about snakes, and it energised her to be on her own for a bit, breathing the pungent Australian mountain air.

The whole place smelt like a congestion remedy, very different but unexpectedly pleasant and fresh. Her spirits rose, and she felt zestfully curious and happy to be alive. She could see how dry everything was, though. Bark and desiccated leaves crunched beneath her feet on the trail. The little river that gurgled over round, ochre-toned rocks was obviously lower than usual, and she began to understand the tongue-clicking and head-shaking she'd encountered in a few locals since her arrival yesterday.

'We really need the rain,' shuttle bus drivers and desk clerks and Australian pulmonary specialists all said obsessively.

Alison had her own obsession this evening. Every time she heard footsteps approaching through the crackling vegetation of the loop trail, she launched into a fantasy—or possibly a waking nightmare—that she would come face to face with Nico around a sudden bend. She'd gasp. He'd grab her elbows to steady her, but she wouldn't need him to, because she'd be steady and strong already.

She would then come out with the most lucid, cutting, fluent, to-the-point speech she'd ever made in her life about what had happened between them seven years ago.

Thank you, Nico, for proving that it's safer to keep to what I know. Thank you for not prolonging the pain with a drawn-out break-up. Thank you for giving such a boost to my career. You should have seen how I hid myself in work and study that year! Hint for the future, though, with the next woman—give her some small clue about *why*.

Although if she was totally honest with herself, she had a pretty good idea...

And don't let it happen in Italy, because Italy is too beautiful a backdrop for such a critical body blow. Italy is made for romance, not heartbreak, and you're a...expletive deleted...for dealing me the body blow there.

Finally, she would leave him propped in a metaphorical gibbering heap against a eucalyptus tree, to be rescued hours later by a park ranger, all that emotional literacy of his exposed like an undressed wound.

It didn't happen, of course.

He wasn't on the trail.

She got back to her room at seven-thirty, ready for a soak in the bath, and heard the first distant rumble of thunder just as she opened her door. By eight, the storm sounded as if it was almost overhead, and she kept expecting the rain that all the locals were so desperate about—a barrage of the stuff drumming on the hotel roof and in the parking lot, drowning the thirsty vegetation.

As with Niccolo Conti's fantasised appearance on the nature walk, however, it didn't happen. Lightning crackled with fluorescent intensity in the air, and the steep sides of the mountain valley made the thunder echo violently back and forth, but barely a drop of rain fell.

After her bath, Alison's jet lag overtook her and she dropped into a deep, sudden sleep with the sound of the dry storm still strong in her ears. When she awoke next morning at around six, she could smell smoke in the air.

At breakfast in the hotel's main restaurant—she'd asked for a corner table, and sat defensively with her back to the wall, which she would probably laugh at herself about later—she questioned her waiter. Were there forest fires in the area? Was it anything to worry about?

'Couple of fires got started during the storm last night, I've heard,' he answered. 'Lightning strikes. They're well to the west and north of us, nothing to worry about, even though we're getting the smoke. Firies might have a rough time getting to them, though.'

'Fierys?' Was that what he'd said?

'Volunteer bushfire brigade. The New South Wales Rural Fire Service.'

'Oh, right…'

'It's wilderness country, you see, hardly any roads to give access for the crews. Not your concern, though. Conference ends Saturday, doesn't it? After the dinner?'

'That's right.'

'Enjoying it so far?'

'Yes, thanks. Very much.'

Except when I think about that tall Italian man who's just walked in and is pretending, again, that he never looked in my direction…

Who is more afraid of whom here?

'I'll have the, um, just coffee and an English muffin, please.'

Again, it wasn't funny.

The smoke in the air grew thicker and stronger during

the course of the day, and a couple of people said they'd seen fire trucks going past on the main road above the village. Alison went to the morning conference sessions and gave her own paper on 'Pre- and Post-Natal Factors in Chronic Lung Disease' in the afternoon, with no pulmonology joke included. Despite this omission, it seemed to go well.

Seeking the fresh air and solitude she'd enjoyed yesterday in order to wind down afterwards, she found the whole atmosphere beyond the air-conditioned conference rooms very different now. When she'd arrived on Wednesday afternoon, the lines of the mountain range had been etched sharply against a gorgeous sky, almost as blue as a china glaze. Now they'd softened behind an ugly grey-brown pall whose smell oppressed the air.

Alison automatically thought about respiratory problems—asthma and allergies and chronic obstructive pulmonary disease, all of which would be exacerbated in many patients by the smoke particles in the atmosphere. There had to be a medical clinic here. Was it equipped to deal with these conditions?

As the breakfast waiter had told her this morning, however, it wasn't her concern.

She had plenty of other things on her mind.

Not Niccolo Conti.

He was peripheral.

Irrelevant.

Done and gone from her life, long ago. She had no intention of going anywhere near the conference suite where Conti Pharmaceuticals had set up a display of its latest drugs and high-tech medical equipment, and this wasn't lack of courage on her part, she told herself, it was simple common sense.

Why complicate her life? She worked hard to stay in the

top rank of her profession, and her mother worked harder, which wasn't right at her age and made Alison worry as she attempted to share some of her mother's load. She'd tried to persuade Mom to come out here with her for the conference and a good break for both of them after it—a week of lying on a beach in the sun.

But Mom remained as driven as ever and wouldn't come. She ran her own contract office cleaning company now, after working at the lowliest level in that industry for years, and she didn't know how to delegate, so Alison was having her week at the beach on her own.

It couldn't come fast enough.

Sunday.

She only had to wait two more days.

The prospect of tomorrow's conference sessions didn't appeal—neither did the dinner tomorrow night, but at least the keynote speaker looked interesting. Maybe she'd hide in her room during the day, and only venture out in the evening.

Or maybe…

The hotel was offering an all-day mini-bus tour package for tomorrow, intended for conference spouses and other visiting tourists and taking in some of the highlights of the surrounding national park. There was a wildlife sanctuary which promised kangaroos and koalas, a hydro-electric power station which might be more interesting than it sounded, a guided cave exploration and a wilderness swimming pool fed by a natural thermal spring.

Bring your togs! said the brochure. Her swimsuit, she mentally translated. Towels were provided, as was a picnic lunch.

She asked about the tour at the concierge desk. 'I'm thinking of goofing off tomorrow. Is there still space available? Will it go ahead with the current fire situation?'

'Yes, to both,' the desk clerk said cheerfully. 'The bush-fires are miles away, and containment lines are in place, but a couple of people have cancelled because of the smoke haze. I'm not making any guarantees on your mountain views, but the other attractions won't be affected. Pretty nice to be in a cool cave or a balmy thermal pool, I would think.'

Yes, it would.

'Sold!' she told him, smiling, and booked and paid for one of the two remaining seats then and there.

She didn't find out until she boarded the bus the next morning that another conference attendee had had the same idea.

Nico.

OK, yes, *now* it was funny.

Almost.

In a God-has-a-sense-of-humour kind of way.

They'd spent the past two days diligently pretending the other didn't exist, only to discover that they'd paid good money for eight hours together on an eleven-seater mini-bus. There were three empty places left when Alison climbed aboard. She chose the one next to Nico, because to do anything else at this point would have been…just silly. He watched her approach the way a Buddhist monk might watch the approach of an asteroid on a collision course with planet Earth—with fatalistic acceptance of the cosmic joke.

'I should have come up and said hello to you at the opening reception on Thursday evening,' she said, skipping anything like 'Hi, Nico' as being superfluous at this stage.

A gust of rising wind buffeted the side of the mini-bus as she took her seat. Weather conditions were atrocious this morning. That smoke haze was thicker and uglier in colour, and it was going to be hot. Forty degrees in nearby Canberra, she'd seen on the early morning news.

What did that translate to in Fahrenheit? Above the cen-

tury mark, she thought, glad of her sand-coloured shorts and
strappy black top. Her feet were already hot in their cotton
socks and walking shoes, and she was glad she'd brought
sunscreen and a brimmed hat.

'Then why didn't you?' Nico asked.

He didn't favour her with his smile, but it hovered somewhere in the background. Just her memory of it maybe. Its
warmth. Its sense of secret understanding. Close up, his eyes
also had the same power and intensity and heat that she
remembered so well.

You really had to look hard to determine what colour they
were. Not green. Not brown. A darkened and exotic mix of
topaz and jade, like the names Charlotte Goodwin wanted
for a daughter.

'Probably the same reason that you didn't,' she answered
him, after a silence that hung in the air three seconds too
long. She had time to realise that she didn't feel nearly as
bad about confronting him now that it had actually happened. Her senses were on full alert, yes, but her stomach
wasn't churning. The blood wasn't pounding in her head.

He was very casually dressed today, in a white T-shirt,
jeans and hiking boots, and there was a leather day-pack
resting at his feet. The T-shirt was a little loose, and somehow this only made Alison more aware of the body beneath
it.

It suggested his laid-back yet confident attitude. He didn't
need to parade his six-pack and his pecs with a skin-tight
fit. He could afford to be similarly casual about every one
of his many assets.

'And what reason is that?' His soft accent made the words
into less of a challenge than they would have been in her
own voice.

He sat back in his seat as he spoke, leaning his strong
shoulder against the window. But the seats weren't generous

in width and she could still feel the warmth and pressure of his hip and thigh. To cut the contact, she would have had to perch with unnatural stiffness too far to the left.

'Oh, don't!' she said, not managing to keep distress out of her voice now. 'You know! All the reasons. All the awkwardness. Everything.'

'The whole misguided fiasco of our relationship,' he murmured, and even after all this time it hurt her to think that he would refer to it like that.

Seven years ago, she'd been so starry-eyed about what she'd thought they had.

She'd felt so very different...

CHAPTER TWO

'DON'T blow this chance, honey,' Doretta Lane told her daughter. 'It's so important.'

'Important? Well, yes.'

More so than she wanted to let on to her mother.

'Meeting Niccolo's family, and on their own ground. He wouldn't have asked you if he wasn't serious about you, but don't forget that for him it's a test.'

Which wasn't the kind of importance Alison had been thinking of.

'It has to be,' her mother went on. 'With his family background, his assets, he could have practically any girl he wants, and if he wants you, seriously, long term, then you *have* to make the right impression on his family. You'll be on trial every waking moment. It's not going to be easy.'

She hugged Alison fiercely.

'I can't believe it! My daughter and the Conti Pharmaceuticals heir. I wouldn't even have dared dream about something like this. I've worked so hard for you, and you've been such a wonderful daughter. When you got into medical school, now, *that* was a dream come true, but this…!'

'Mom, stop!' Alison felt rattled by her mother's fast, almost feverish words, and by the content that lay behind them as well.

She never thought of Nico the way Mom did—that he was a 'catch' she couldn't have dreamed of, that he had 'assets' she should be awed by, that she needed to make 'the right impression'.

He always seemed so natural and casual—just a warm, good, perceptive human being—and their relationship had evolved so easily during their just-completed internship year at a highly regarded hospital in Central Ohio. A medical intern's workload didn't allow for too much formality with one's fellows. You felt like soldiers together on the front lines, and both comradeship and hostility could build quickly.

Nico's good looks had struck her almost from the beginning.

How could they not?

But, then, he made funny mistakes with his English sometimes, and he griped about the same senior doctors as she did, he dreaded the same difficult cases and had the same rumpled, bleary-eyed appearance when he was roused from an exhausted sleep in the junior on-call room, and she couldn't be in awe of him.

He made her laugh, he had a smile that arrowed right to her heart, he brought her coffee in the middle of the night, he knew at once when she was particularly on edge or particularly in doubt of her skills, he always reassured her or teased her out of it, and she trusted him—trusted him with her whole heart.

It had been weeks before she'd found out he was ridiculously wealthy, heir to a huge corporation and saddled with an aristocratic Italian pedigree that went back a good four centuries.

He hadn't made a big deal out of any of it, because he didn't want anyone else to, so pretty soon she didn't consider that it *was* a big deal. When he'd asked her to spend four weeks of the summer with him in Italy to meet his family, all she'd thought about at first had been him.

That was why the trip to Italy seemed important.

Because she'd be with him, in one of the most romantic places in the world.

Italian food, Mediterranean beaches and Nico. Warm summer nights, splashing rococo fountains, and her tender, wonderful lover. A whole new world to discover, completely outside her experience but vivid in her imagination. Red wine, moonlight, *no patients* threatening to sneakily take a turn for the worse just when the senior resident was due to show up and look with critical eyes over the notes that recorded the treatment she'd given…no patients and no stress, just Nico.

Her mother's tense attitude tarnished her anticipation and brought her back to earth.

Was it such a big deal?

Was she really on trial?

Was this not about her and Nico and wider horizons at all?

'You'll need clothes,' Mom said. 'Good clothes. It doesn't matter about jewellery, we can't pretend we're something we're not, but you can't look like a frump or an embarrassment.'

'Nice if we could afford for me not to!'

Alison's mother pressed her lips together. 'I'll just have to take out a personal loan. It won't be for much. Just a couple of thousand dollars. Three.'

'Three thousand dollars for clothes? No, Mom!'

'It's pocket change, on top of your student loans for medical school.'

'There's a point to those.'

And they were massive. Even on a doctor's rapidly climbing income, Alison would need years to pay them off. She dreamed about them sometimes, and woke up in a sweat with vague memories of chasing dollar bills down a windy street and never ever catching them.

'There's a point to this,' her mother said. 'You have to look right, and sound right, and act right. I wonder if a quick course in modelling and etiquette before you go...'

'No!'

Alison refused to consider any of her mother's wilder suggestions, but some damage had already been done. She felt more and more nervous about the trip as it got closer, and wished that Nico wasn't going a week ahead of her. When she was actually with him, she never felt like this. He always teased her out of the tense emotional knots she could get herself into. He yanked her right out of her comfort zone and laughed while he was doing it so that soon she was laughing, too. It would have been much easier to travel together.

It would have been easier not to travel first class!

She was seated next to a cool Italian blonde wearing an immaculate suit and very expensive shoes, and even though 'next to' in first class meant five feet away, the woman still spooked her with questions to the flight attendants about the wine list and the food that Alison herself wouldn't have remotely known how to ask.

The human circulatory and respiratory systems, fine. Back to front and inside out. She could almost have written the textbook.

Wine? It came in three colours, red, white and the occasional pink, and that's all she knew.

The blonde gave off an aura of familiarity with being waited on, as if it was her absolute birthright. Her smiles were courteous yet arctic and she seemed profoundly bored.

Is that how I'm supposed to act? Is that how I'm supposed to *feel*?

By the time the flight landed in Rome, Alison's stomach was fluttering with nerves, and it didn't help that Niccolo had brought his mother with him, although he obviously meant well by it. Alison already knew what a strong sense of duty and family he had.

Mom's right, she found herself thinking. This *is* a test. I have to live up to what his parents will be looking for.

The blonde on the plane had disappeared into the aircraft bathroom when the flight reached the European coast, to emerge an hour later with her make-up completely redone and her suit accessorised with different jewellery. All Alison had thought to bring in her carry-on bag were her toothbrush, her hairbrush and her mascara.

And Nico's mother looked more like the blonde than she looked like her son's girlfriend. Her smile seemed genuine, but her hug was stiff and short, and there was a definite glance down at Alison's outfit of tailored trousers and cotton top. Thank goodness she'd listened to Mom on that one and hadn't worn nice comfortable stretch jeans!

Faustina Conti said something long and sort of *rippling* in Italian, then translated it herself at once into fluent though accented English, without the accompanying smile that the words needed. 'How good it is to meet you! We have been surprised that Nico would bring you, but our surprise quickly turned to pleasure, my dear, and now already I am utterly charmed!'

Beside her, Nico rolled his eyes and grinned, and Alison had to struggle not to emit a nervous laugh. 'Sounds much better in Italian,' he murmured in her ear as they turned to walk towards the baggage claim area. He took her hand secretly in his, as if he'd known just how much she needed it, and she felt a rush of relief and happiness.

Then she thought back on the bit about the Conti family being 'surprised that Nico would bring you'.

'So you hadn't said much to them about me, then?' she asked him, her tone timid.

'No, not really. I didn't want to make it into a big deal. You know how it is.'

Did she? She wasn't sure about that.

'It's delightful to meet you, too, Mrs Conti,' she told his mother, a little slower with the reply than good manners required.

And she never normally used the word delightful. It sounded pretentious and unnatural coming out of her mouth, leaving an odd taste, and when she waited for Faustina Conti to invite her to call her by her first name, the invitation didn't come.

Other invitations did, however, in the days that followed.

Lots of them.

Too many.

The moonlight walks, and the plates of pasta shared in little corner bistros, and kissing Nico on the beach didn't happen nearly enough, not nearly as much as Alison had dreamed about. Instead, there were elegant dinners with Conti Pharmaceuticals executives and their wives, and outings on the luxury family motor cruiser in which she was supposed to loll about in a topless bikini working on her tan and drinking champagne.

Nico's father, Antonio, made it clear that even the boating trips were an obligation more than a pleasure. He seemed bad-tempered, judgmental and distant, and Alison couldn't warm to him.

'He's not himself this summer, I don't know what his problem is, I'm sorry,' Nico said to her, during one of the rare times when they managed to sneak away for some time to themselves. 'I owe him this time here, though.'

Alison's skin didn't tan, she didn't like champagne before sundown, and she couldn't quite shake her American Mid-West modesty about the topless thing, even though she tried. She knew she should be getting more relaxed each day in this environment, as she got to know the extended Conti family better, but instead she felt herself getting stiffer and more nervous, and the stiffer she got, the more unnatural her manner became.

Nico started frowning in her direction when he thought she wasn't looking. He asked her a couple of strange questions about what she valued in life. He didn't seem to like her answers, and she couldn't blame him because she'd felt put on the spot, frozen under a searchlight, *on trial*, just like her mother had said, and she knew she hadn't sounded sincere.

Was she really up to this? she began to wonder. The world she'd grown up in had been so different. If Nico's parents had judged her and found her wanting, maybe they were right.

She began to count the days until she and Nico were due to leave together for the US. She would be starting her residency in Ohio, and he was taking some specialised classes in pharmacology in preparation for his future role in the family company.

He'd originally planned to move to New York for those, but had recently transferred his enrolment back to Ohio, and she knew it was because of her. At times during the past few months she'd wondered if he might rebel against the executive career path that had been planned for him in the Conti corporation, and end up following a medical specialty that lay closer to his heart instead. He was a caring doctor, and patients instinctively trusted him—he'd be good in family practice or paediatrics.

She'd also wondered if he would suggest that they live together this year.

Get married even.

More moonlight and a Mediterranean summer night. How could she not have dreamed about a proposal in Italy?

But the proposal hadn't happened yet, and she wasn't really surprised. The atmosphere wasn't right here, although it surely should have been. Maybe if Nico's father didn't so obviously dislike her…

Once Alison and Nico were on their own in America again, plunged back into their medical careers, would they be able to return to the relaxed relationship they'd had before? Or was Nico's sense of duty too strong?

Subconsciously, Alison began to wait for the blow to fall, and finally it did.

Nico closed up. He no longer acted as if they shared a delicious secret, as if he knew her better than she knew herself. He no longer even tried to snatch any time alone together with her. And he wouldn't explain why.

One day, she took a big breath and tried to ask. 'I'm feeling that we're not connecting the way we did before. It's because I wasn't raised to live this way, isn't it? I'm not used to the…the wealth, and the—But I could learn, Nico,' she told him too eagerly. 'I want to learn.'

He didn't seem to appreciate the suggestion. He closed up even more, wouldn't talk about it, and over the next few days she kept trying, in all sorts of ways, because she just couldn't believe it was all going so sour and bad so fast, after what they'd had so recently at home.

She tried befriending his mother—tried too hard, probably. She tried asking his father about the heritage value of the artwork and furniture and porcelain that graced the family's seventeenth-century home. She tried to sit and move with the cool elegance of Faustina herself and the blonde on the plane. She was meticulous about her clothes and her manners, and extravagant—gushing, at times, in hindsight—about the wonderful food and wine.

She even tried flirting with Nico's older cousin, Massimo, who was a flagrant womaniser, because maybe if Nico could

see that another man found her attractive and didn't consider
her out of place, he'd remember why he did, too.

Note to self—flirting is not your best thing.

Only nine more days went her mantra on the day she and
Nico had their huge, horrible scene, late in the afternoon. It
was the sort of thing that you thought you'd remember every
word of for the rest of your life while it was actually happening. Only ten minutes later, however, when she was sobbing in her room with a swollen face and throbbing eyes,
she'd already lost track of just how it had gone.

It might not have lasted nearly as long as it had seemed
to.

'I can't see any alternative, Alison. I think you had better
cut things short and go home.' She would remember that
part! The lines ran in her head, over and over.

But how had it gone after that?

Oh, yes, she'd asked him why. Of course. She'd wailed
it. 'Wh-y-y?' Oh, she must have looked and sounded—

Pull yourself together, Alison.

And he'd said something about her performance breaking
down under more rigorous conditions. For a fleeting moment she thought she'd seen an odd, lost sort of look on his
face, but that couldn't have been right, not with those words
of his.

'I'm not good enough for your parents, then,' she'd said,
because it had to be that.

'You're not good enough for me! I thought you were…'
Pause. Head shake. 'Different. Not like this. Look, it's probably my fault, too.' A variation on the classic 'It's not you,
it's me' line that no one, male or female, ever really meant.
'I don't think we should see each other again, Alison.'

And even though the Italian trip had been difficult from
the word go, she'd still been stunned. Too stunned to keep
her dignity. Through the wild tears that had started she'd

said things she didn't mean—about his father's influence, about a couple of the topless girls on the boat.

Why had she said those things?

'I don't think we should go on with this discussion,' he'd cut in. 'I'll change your flight tonight, and you'll be able to leave tomorrow afternoon. Start packing now, if you want. I'll find something to tell my parents, and I'll bring a snack to your room so you don't have to come down.'

'I'm not hungry. How could I possibly be hungry?'

'Well, all the same.' He wouldn't even look at her. 'I'll leave it on a tray outside your door.'

And it arrived as promised, announced by the tinkle of crockery just outside the room, while she was still sobbing her heart out and trying to make their confrontation, and their whole vacation, come out differently in her head. If only she hadn't tried so hard. If only they'd had more time together.

A snack for her supper. He was true to his word, even in a situation like this, when he obviously didn't want to lay eyes on her again. She waited until his footsteps retreated— they were definitely his, not the housekeeper's—calmed her sobs, then went to pick up the tray.

There was a note on it. 'I've changed the flight. Massimo will drive you to the airport. You'll need to be ready by noon.'

She cried herself into a dismal sleep and didn't see Nico the next morning.

CHAPTER THREE

ALISON hadn't seen Niccolo Conti in seven years, until that glimpse across the hotel lobby two days ago.

He'd left his mark on her, though. She'd had relationships since. With men who were nothing like Nico but who had a lot in common with herself, at least outwardly—doctors who'd grown up in big American cities and had had to work hard to earn their success. One of the relationships had lasted a year and a half.

But she'd never given her heart in quite the same way, and no man had ever been able to coax it from her, as Nico's instinctive skill had done. They'd been tense, competitive relationships mostly, with the right boundaries and rules in place. She'd always held something back, stayed safe, and she'd never had that wonderful sense of blossoming adventure that her time with Nico had given her.

In hindsight, she knew that not all of the mistakes had been his. She just wished he could have given her more of a chance, forgiven her a little more, because she knew, still, that she'd have forgiven him so much.

Now she was sitting beside him, on the far side of the world, with the hydro-electric power station their first stop on the tour.

An older couple peered into the mini-bus and surveyed the two remaining seats, which were located one behind the other in the second and third rows. 'This is no good, Jerry,' announced the wife. 'They're not next to each other.'

'Does that matter?' he answered, and Alison could immediately hear the evidence of chronic lung problems in his wheezy, bubbly breathing. He couldn't be enjoying these weather conditions. 'We'll be in and out of the bus all day.'

'We should be able to sit together,' his wife insisted.

'How about if I move back a row?' Alison offered.

'Oh, would you, dear?'

'It's no trouble at all.' She didn't look at Nico. He wouldn't have let any relief show on his face, but he probably felt it as strongly as she did. No need to sit side by side now, and yet they hadn't had to openly avoid each other either.

Except that she didn't want to avoid him, she suddenly discovered.

She wanted to be civilised about this, and a little brave, to prove to herself and to him that she'd moved on long ago. Avoidance or open hostility would suggest that he was still...well...*important* in some way, and he wasn't. After seven years, he didn't matter a bit. He couldn't possibly.

She should have realised that two days ago, and she should have greeted Nico the way she'd have greeted any one-time colleague she hadn't seen in that long. In hindsight, she was a little surprised that he hadn't done the same thing himself, for exactly the reasons she'd arrived at now—their total lack of importance in each other's lives.

'Jerry, let her have some space to move,' the wife scolded. 'She can't do it with you crowding in like that.'

'No, no, I'm fine.' Alison slipped out of the seat and moved back.

The husband climbed aboard, but this turned out to be no good either. The wife didn't want a window seat because looking out of it at that angle might give her motion sickness. They swapped places so that she could sit in the centre, and her sizeable handbag bumped Nico's knee several times in the process, although apparently she didn't notice this even when he angled his legs more sharply towards the side of the vehicle.

'Valda!' Jerry scolded her vaguely, as he heaved in another breath.

Alison found herself feeling thankful this was an eight-hour day trip, not a three-week European trek. She saw Nico give the wife a nod and smile that already seemed to contain a wealth of understanding about how the older woman should be handled.

'Please, let me know if you are not comfortable,' he murmured, and then casually turned to study the view from the window.

He got out his digital camera and started experimenting with different settings, absorption showing in his face as if the camera was new to him and he didn't fully understand it yet. The message that he didn't want to talk, though tactfully expressed, came through loud and clear and Alison couldn't stop a little smile which she hoped no one saw.

In the right hands—Nico's hands—cameras were useful for more than just taking pictures.

The mini-bus was full now. A very youthful-looking tour guide jumped into the driver's seat and threw a cheery 'Morning, folks!' over his shoulder. He took a quick roll call, referring to a folded print out pulled from his pocket. 'Sarah and Troy Field?'

'That's us,' said the attractive young couple next to Alison.

'Don't worry,' the driver told them in a stage whisper. 'I won't let anyone know you're on your honeymoon.'

A few people laughed.

'Midori Hiromichi? Yes? Good.' Alison recognised the last name of the very well-regarded Japanese paediatric lung specialist who'd presented a paper at the conference yesterday morning. This was apparently his wife, sitting quietly alone in the back corner of the vehicle. Her knowledge of English didn't seem to go beyond a few words.

'Edwin Chaffey?'

'Present, sir,' the overweight man in the front passenger seat replied in a schoolboy squeak. A couple of people laughed at this, too.

'Jerry and Valda Lister… Joan Bright… Deirdre Searle… Alison Lane… Nico Conti… All here. And I'm Sam. So let's go.'

Sam had a pleasant, competent tour-guide patter, containing a mixture of facts about the area as well as some lame jokes he'd obviously learned by heart. Alison didn't listen to much of what he said. She was too busy watching the hot, desiccating wind.

It really was horrible today, tearing through the tall, supple trees until she thought it would rip the leaves right off the branches. She saw long strips of bark whipping through the air or littering the road, and once a branch at least two inches thick came clattering down onto the verge just as they drove past.

Behind her, Joan and Deirdre made some uneasy comments to each other.

'The caves will be nice today.'

'Sheltered.'

The power station wasn't bad either. Security had been heightened in recent years, so they weren't taken past the turbines, but the display in the public area of the building had some interesting features.

Alison forced herself to go up to Nico. 'This whole Snowy Mountains hydro-electricity project must have been a mammoth undertaking.'

Ten points, Alison. A nice, dry remark, not hostile, yet as neutral and impersonal as possible. Just the tone she wanted to take.

But Nico quirked one eyebrow as if he wasn't impressed. A little amused, ready to tease, but definitely not impressed.

'I thought when you first got on the bus that we might have been headed for a slightly more stimulating exchange than that, Dr Lane.' He sounded just the same as he used to, his English fast and fluent and confident, laced with Italian rhythms, American vowels and a talent for humour that crossed cultural boundaries and invited her to share.

'Stimulating?' she echoed. 'You mean you want to discuss medicine? The conference?'

He laughed. 'No. Don't be obtuse. Isn't it traditional in this situation to ask barbed and supposedly casual questions about each other's more recent lovers—?'

'What?'

'In the hope of discovering evidence of some shocking scandal or embarrassing failure that would prove we were well rid of one another?'

'I don't know,' Alison said bluntly. 'You tell me. Is it? Remember, I'm not good at this stuff.'

European etiquette, she meant. Aristocratic double standards. Put-downs disguised as compliments. Rules of conduct that people like the Contis absorbed in childhood the way their picturesque *palazzo* in Venice—their second residence—absorbed rising damp.

Nico frowned at her answer, and the teasing look left his face. 'No, perhaps you are not,' he said. 'I'll ask, then. Are you married? Divorced? A parent?'

'None of the above.'

'I'm surprised.'

'Sometimes, so am I,' she blurted out. 'The plan was different at one time.'

Oh, lord, where had that come from?

Yes, she'd always assumed that marriage and children lay in her future. She no longer assumed that, but she still hoped. She just wasn't quite sure how fate would manage to trick her into it, that was all, when she was so careful and insufficiently brave.

Nico waited, using the old ruse of letting his silence draw her into further speech. It worked like a charm, because she felt stupidly nervous and fluttery this close to him, and the cool control and distance she'd been trying for had fled.

'I mean because most women…most doctors…at my level are,' she said, 'married or divorced or—Are you?'

'Like you, none of the above. My lifestyle hasn't permitted it, at this stage.'

He allowed himself a small, gorgeous grimace of regret which Alison didn't take seriously for a second. The phrase 'my lifestyle' suggested bachelor pads in New York and Rome and hotel suites all over the world, as well as smooth apologies to a succession of beautiful women, along the lines of, 'I'm sorry, I'm flying to Europe tomorrow, but when I get back next month…'

Her own dismissal from his life hadn't been smoothly made, though, she remembered. He'd been oddly emotional and awkward in the lengths he'd gone to not to encounter her again before her flight, with those hesitant footsteps, that tray left by her door and that abrupt note.

In Ohio, he'd never turned up for his pharmacology studies. The admissions office wouldn't give her any information, understandably, but she could only assume he'd transferred back to New York. She'd desperately hoped for a phone call that would spell out his change of heart, or tell her he loved her after all, that he understood why she'd been so awkward in Italy, that it was his feelings that counted, not his parents' wishes, but it hadn't happened, and after a few weeks she'd realised it wasn't going to.

'Tell me about your lifestyle,' she said. 'Your life, I

mean,' she revised at once. 'You're full time with Conti now? Not practising medicine at all?'

'That's right.' He gave a short nod. 'The Debentech acquisition has been a major deal. I won't bore you with the details, but it's been a while since I've had a stethoscope around my neck.'

'Do you ever wonder whether all those years of study were a waste? Couldn't you have joined the family firm at the same level without a medical background?'

She heard a breath escape between his teeth that almost sounded like a sigh.

'On paper, yes, of course,' he said. 'But the medical degree wasn't just something to bolster my résumé against whispered accusations of nepotism from more junior executives. It was something I'd always wanted to do, and it fulfilled several goals. I hope that I will practise again at some stage. My father and I have talked about it.'

'He'd be happy?' This wasn't the impression she'd had in Italy seven years ago.

'He'd understand my reasons.'

'Neatly sidestepped, Dr Conti.'

One corner of his mouth turned up. 'It was, wasn't it?'

'You're good at that, I'm sure.'

'I've had a bit of practice.'

'How are your parents?' Alison heard herself ask, and for some reason her most vivid memories of them, as she spoke, were the best ones—the way they enjoyed a big family meal, the way they exaggerated the anecdotes they told and expected their listeners to sort out truth from fiction for themselves.

'They're good, at the moment,' Nico answered. His voice dropped a little. 'Although my father—'

'Everybody…back…on…the…bus!' Cutting loudly across Nico's words, Edwin had his hands shaped like a megaphone and his voice contorted into a weird kind of British accent. Cockney, or something. Alison guessed he must be quoting from a classic movie or television show, but she didn't get the reference. She didn't have a lot of time to keep her popular culture education up to date.

But she did know a fair bit about human beings. Edwin obviously considered himself the class clown and was happy in the role.

'What were you saying about your father, Nico?' Alison asked.

He shook his head. 'Not now. He was ill after you left Italy, that's all. That's why he was in such a foul mood that summer, although we didn't know at the time.'

Sam strolled up to the group. 'Doing my job for me, Mr Chaffey?'

'Just call me Eddie.'

'Thanks, then, Eddie. Yes, we do have to get a wriggle on, if we're going to fit in a swim at the thermal pool.'

'Is that next?' Joan asked, with Deirdre nodding at her side. Apparently the phrase 'get a wriggle on' made perfect sense to them.

The two women were aged somewhere in their mid-seventies, Alison guessed. Both were widows, as they'd already mentioned, but they were apparently determined not to be stuck at home because of it. They'd been friends since school.

'No, the caves are next,' Sam said. 'Then we'll drive down to the pool, where we'll have our picnic lunch and a swim for those who want one.'

They drove for another forty-five minutes to reach the complex of limestone caves, and the tour took an hour and a half. The sense of relief at being out of the wind and heat was immense, and even Valda, who had complained about several more small problems since her fuss over the seating

at the start of the tour, seemed awed by the beautiful for-
mations.

Alison caught the young honeymoon pair kissing in the
dark at one point, before their cave guide turned on the next
series of lights, but she kept the discovery to herself, where
Sam or Edwin Chaffey might have teased them about it.

'Feeling OK, sweetheart?' Troy whispered.

'No, queasy and revolting as usual,' Sarah whispered
back. 'Mum was right. Pregnant brides should postpone the
honeymoon until the second trimester.'

Near the end of the tour, Alison accidentally bumped into
Nico during another interval of dimness, and their bare arms
touched. It was chilly in the cave and she shivered. The
light dusting of dark hair on his forearm had tickled her,
and had reminded her of how thoroughly masculine he was,
despite his urbane European veneer. His body wouldn't have
matched the waxed appearance of a male model in a magazine. He gave her a sharp look at their moment of contact,
and she moved away as quickly as she could.

Was the weather even worse when they emerged, or had
they just forgotten the intensity of the heat and wind while
protected by the blessed silence and coolness of the cave?
The smoke haze seemed thicker, and Alison wasn't surprised to hear Valda throwing some sharp questions at her
husband about his medication. He told her he was fine, but
Nico, who'd also overheard, didn't looked convinced.

'What do you usually take? What have you brought with
you?' he asked. 'You see, I'm a doctor. I have a strong
knowledge of pharmaceuticals, and I have one or two things
with me that might be of use. Do let me know if you're
concerned.'

'He's only got his inhaler. The other things are back at
the hotel,' Valda answered for her husband.

'But it's rubbish, anyhow,' Jerry said. 'I don't need any of it. There's nothing wrong with me.'

Alison had met his type before. Such patients were very hard to help. Nico would have picked up on this, too.

'In which directions are the fires?' she asked Sam.

He gestured vaguely towards the next ridge of mountains, and repeated what several people had now said. 'Miles away.' After a second or two, he revised, 'This wind will be bringing the fire fronts closer, though. If they jump the containment lines…'

'The wind seems very changeable. It's not blowing steadily from one direction.'

'No. You're right. It's clocking around though, oh, a hundred and twenty degrees, south-west to west to north. That'll make it all harder to keep under control.'

'Are you local? Have you seen fires through here before?'

'No, I'm from Sydney.' She must have looked doubtful, because he added in a stout tone, 'But of course I'm fully trained in client safety and first aid. It's pretty much common-sense stuff. Stay with the vehicle. Get down low. Not that we'll need to do any of that. Let's hit our picnic spot, then I'll try and retune the radio, see if they're broadcasting any warnings.'

'I don't like the sound of that!'

'The park rangers will keep us posted. They closed one section of the park last night, but that's—'

'I know. Miles away,' she finished for him, on a drawl.

'They're on top of this, Dr Lane, they really are.'

'I guess you're right. They would surely close the park, wouldn't they?' She'd seen several uniformed park rangers, as well as their own cave guide, and there were other tourists about. Nobody looked as if they were enjoying the conditions, but nobody was panicking either.

Their group boarded the mini-bus once more, and Sam

drove the short distance to the parking area that served the thermal pool and picnic facilities, at the end of a hundred-metre walk.

'Swim or eat, in whichever order you want,' he said. 'We have gourmet sandwiches here, cheese and crackers, fruit, cake, champagne, mineral water and fruit juice. And the picnic shelter should protect us from the wind.'

It didn't, really. The wind was too strong and too variable for that. Most people ate first, and no one lingered over their lunch. Alison didn't feel hungry in the heat, so she was one of the first to put on her swimsuit and seek the refreshment of the pool. Built into the lee of some steeply sloping rocks, it was more sheltered than the picnic place had been and the water felt like milk, just cool enough to give her a boost of energy.

She swam up and down, and realised how much she'd missed the swim and exercise routine she hadn't gotten to for at least a week before flying out here, because she'd been working her way through the usual massive 'to do' list that she always seemed to generate before any kind of a break.

A break…

She'd be flying up to Byron Bay tomorrow, hours from this wind and dryness and heat, hours from fellow lung specialists, hours from Niccolo Conti, hours from all the ways he'd suddenly confronted her with her own past. It didn't seem real at the moment.

He didn't seem real, not even when he appeared in front of her, powering down the pool at a strong crawl, putting in his twenty or thirty laps just the way she was.

They must both be too driven, she decided as they passed each other. The Listers weren't swimming at all, and neither were Eddie or Mrs Hiromichi. Joan and Deirdre only bobbed cautiously at one end of the pool, and even the honeymooners just lolled in each other's arms in the water and splashed a bit. Several strangers seemed similarly relaxed.

Nico caught up to her as she rested a little breathlessly at the deep end, and she said to him on an impulse, 'What are we trying to prove, I wonder?'

Even now, there was an odd way in which she found him easy to talk to and instinctively expected him to understand. Words just came out, as if the truest part of herself was closer to the surface when he was around.

If he felt remotely the same, it didn't show right now. His handsome, tanned face stiffened, his gaze flicked over her and he didn't smile. 'Nothing. Why would I have anything to prove to you, after so long?'

'Oh, no, I just meant the way we're swimming. No one else is using this pool as a substitute for their regular gym workout, like we are.'

He rolled around to face the pool and ducked his head and shoulders beneath the water once more before he replied. Waiting, Alison held onto the pool's stone edge and watched the way the water streamed from his short dark hair, making it lie flat against his perfectly shaped head.

His legs disappeared down into the green-tinted water, below a pair of loose black swim trunks. The smoky sunlight reflected off the sheen of water on his fine-pored olive skin, reminding her of how he'd looked when they'd swum off the side of the boat in Italy, and his incredible eyes were narrowed against the glare.

'Maybe some of them should,' he said. 'Eddie's not in good shape for his age. I heard him tell Sam that he was fifty-four, but he looks older.'

'Yes, over sixty, I'd have said,' Alison answered.

'And Jerry's left it too late, even if his own attitude to his breathing problems could be worked on.'

'Which is doubtful. Joan and Deirdre are doing well, though.'

They'd both started a decorous breaststroke across the pool at the shallow end. Forty years ago, they'd have been wearing waterproof bathing caps decorated with rubber flowers to protect their salon-styled waves.

'I have the impression they're pretty intrepid,' Nico said, and Alison realised that he'd deflected the conversation topic right away from anything personal between the two of them. Adept of him. They'd reached the safe, familiar area of medicine instead.

She should probably be grateful for that. It was essentially what she'd tried to do herself, back at the power station. They would go their separate ways again in a few hours. It didn't make sense to indulge in any kind of character analysis, let alone any recrimination, any picking over of the past, any discovery of shared regret or relief. They should stick with safer subjects.

'Well, five laps to go,' she told him lightly, and set off again.

Niccolo watched Alison leave the pool and head for the changing rooms after she'd completed her self-imposed lap total, disguising his focus on her with some lazy stretching motions in the water. He was stunned at the way seven years had simply seemed to vanish over the past few hours. Glimpsing her at the conference, having known in advance that she would be there, he'd felt satisfied that after such a passage of time he was immune.

He wasn't, though. He wasn't at all.

Now that he'd been thrown into Alison's company, he could remember that burning, growing, totally unexpected sense of naïvety—of having been fooled—as if he'd felt it just yesterday. He remembered the hurt and anger and confusion, the shock of discovering that he was still a boy when he'd felt himself a man.

Most of all, though, he remembered how good their relationship had seemed to him before the trip home to Italy, and remembered all the things that had attracted him to her from the beginning. Her colouring, so exotic to his eyes—all the clear, perfect blue and white and red-gold of hair and skin and eyes. Like porcelain.

At first he'd expected her to be delicate, cosseted, princess-like because she looked so feminine and slight and soft. But he'd soon realised she wasn't. She was clever, hard-working, determined…and tense. Very tense! Adorably so, he'd always thought.

She disappeared into the changing room at the top of the path, and he discovered that he was grinning at an avalanche of memories.

She'd tied herself into such unnecessary knots about patients, exams, career decisions. She'd never seemed to recognise her own strengths until something happened that left her in no doubt, and even then she'd be so surprised—ambushed by her own feelings. Her own laughter and tears would astonish her. Her courage—and she had a lot of it, although she didn't know that—would seem to her like a miracle falling from the sky.

He'd loved being the one who had the power to show her her own strengths, to loosen the knots, to bring out her confidence.

He hadn't always succeeded, though, he remembered, and that had frustrated him. There had been times when he'd felt he wasn't reaching her, and it wasn't a feeling he liked. He hadn't understood the most secret, hidden source of her tension—the extent of her ambitions—until the trip to Italy, and then it had hit him like a slap across the face.

He remembered a crucial conversation with his father as if it were a film replaying in his head.

'I'm sorry, Dad, I know she's a little awkward. This isn't the kind of environment she's used to, and she tends to get stressed and wound up about things like that.'

'This should tell you something, Nico, surely.'

'That she doesn't fit in? She will, with time.'

'That it's an impossible relationship! We had no idea you were so serious about this girl. Wake up, Nico! Not only is your future with Conti Pharmaceuticals completely incompatible with any career ambitions she may have, it's clear that she is after our money and our name more than anything else. This is the source of her tension. She can tell that your mother and I are under no illusions, and she's frightened that she won't pull off the coup. You watch. You listen.'

'No, Dad! You're wrong.'

'Watch. Listen. Think with your head, and not something lower down. Your mother and I went along with this idea of the medical degree, and we are so proud of your ambition in that area, and what you have achieved. We could not have asked for a better son. But it's time that you listen to us now. I have seen little evidence in the girl's behaviour that suggests she cares for more than the material advantages you can give her. If you respect my opinion at all—'

'Of course I do.'

'Then credit me with some experience in this area, and at least look at her with a cooler eye!'

So he had, and he'd been convinced.

He'd felt the sting for a long time, and it had changed him—changed what he looked for in a relationship—and it had given him the very definite goal of waiting until he was well into his thirties before settling down. At some point, yes, he'd decided seven years ago, he would need a wife and children. It was a duty as much as an emotional drive.

But he was going to wait, pick the right kind of woman, use his head and not expect too much.

He still felt that way.

He did.

He had to.

Because it would be crazy to give the ghost of his long-dead love for Alison Lane the power it seemed to want...

Nico was still churning up and down when Alison had dressed, and she couldn't help pausing just outside the change-room door to look down the path towards him. So strong, so steady, so focused.

And so *sincere*, she would have thought. He wasn't swimming like that to show off those powerful shoulders or that naturally olive skin. He was doing it because it felt good, because he enjoyed his body's strength, and because he wanted the exercise.

This didn't quite jibe with what she'd convinced herself of over the years—that he must really have been shallow and two-faced and manipulative and she just hadn't been mature or experienced enough to see it at the time. The callous womaniser she'd created in her mind in a gesture of self-protection would most definitely have been showing off in the water. And she'd have seen it in the subtleties of his body language, because she was much more experienced now.

I'm crazy, she thought almost feverishly. Am I going to let him get under my skin again so fast? Thank heaven this is just for a few hours.

'We should be making a move,' Sam said to the group gathered in the inadequate protection of the picnic shelter a little later.

He'd come over from the mini-bus, and Nico must have seen him and guessed what he was saying, because he swam at once to the metal ladder at the side of the pool and pulled himself out.

Sam waved at him and everyone looked across, pulling Alison's focus in the same direction. Something coiled and flipped inside her at the sight of Nico's bare torso, shaped like a blunt wedge with its widest point at his shoulders. She'd fallen asleep against that chest more than once. She'd stroked it possessively with her hands. She'd felt unimaginably blessed—just lucky, lucky, lucky—to have the right to consider him and his smile and his heartbeat and his gorgeous brown body hers.

Her secret gift, so deeply treasured, never to be lost.

Only he hadn't felt the same way about her. She'd failed his family's test and he'd lost interest, closed off. If he'd loved her the way she'd thought he did, his family's opinion wouldn't have mattered. He'd never loved her, and she'd been a fool.

'Did you manage to hear anything on the radio?' she turned to ask Sam, before Nico could get close enough to see the way she'd been looking at him.

'No, we must be too far from a signal out here.'

'Oh, that's a pity.'

'We'll try again once we're on the road.'

A National Parks and Wildlife Service vehicle drove across the grass towards them at that moment, and a ranger got out—the guide who'd taken them through the cave.

'We're starting to close the park,' he said. 'Nothing to worry about, it's just a precaution. This wind is lengthening the fire-front and pushing it along faster than predicted. One of the containment lines has been broken and the fire has jumped a road.'

'That doesn't sound good!' Deirdre exclaimed.

'There's some concern, but nothing for you to worry about. If the situation does worsen over the next couple of days, we don't want to have to go chasing people up in isolated camp grounds, that's all.'

'Right.'

'But if you could make your way back to the main gate within the next hour, and check in with the ranger there, let her know I've spoken to you?'

'Right,' Sam said again. 'We're scheduled to head out of here anyhow. Our next stop is a private facility some distance away,' he told the group. 'It's not part of the park.'

They got to the main gate in twenty minutes. The atmosphere in the mini-bus had become a little tense, and Alison felt a rush of unnecessary and illogical relief when Sam slowed to speak to the female ranger and a sign told them they were leaving the park.

She knew the relief didn't make sense. As if the bushfires would respectfully remain behind the park boundary! Much of the country beyond the line of wire fence was just as thickly forested and wild as the park itself. Still, the relief was there, all the same.

Kangaroos and koalas next. That should be fun. You couldn't visit Australia without seeing those.

After finishing his chat with the ranger, Sam drove a few more miles, then pulled onto the verge. 'Let me just check the map,' he said.

'You're not going to get us stuck at a dead-end somewhere, I hope!' Joan teased him. She didn't sound nervous about the possibility, and obviously trusted his expertise. She seemed like a sweet old thing.

'Just refreshing my memory on a short cut,' he answered. 'If they're closing the park, we can't go the usual way, because the road loops back into it for a five-kilometre stretch, and the ranger said just now they'd be putting those orange barriers across at both ends.'

He folded the map again after a moment and set off,

taking a turn to the right and then a second one to the left a few kilometres later, with confident swings of the wheel. The landscape began to look a little less mountainous, and they passed some cleared areas where sheep or cattle grazed.

Sam made a couple more turns. The road he ended up on started out looking fine—sealed and smooth, though narrow—but then the bitumen ended abruptly. 'That's not on the map,' he admitted. 'I'm sure it's OK, though.'

It wasn't. The road got worse and worse.

'Shouldn't we turn back?' Alison asked.

'Americans!' Sam teased her. 'Just because this isn't a six-lane highway.'

It was a rutted track.

'If we don't hit a sign or a turn-off in a couple of k's…' Sam muttered.

They hit a rusty gate. Not literally, thank goodness, but the track unmistakably ended at this point.

'Must have… Let me check the map again.' He unfolded it on the steering-wheel, then leaned on it so that the horn accidentally sounded. Alison and some of the others jumped three feet in the air, and even Nico appeared to flinch. They were all getting tense by this time, and conversation had dwindled to nothing.

'Sorry,' Sam said. He narrowed his eyes over the map for a few minutes, then announced, 'OK, I see what's happened…'

He turned the mini-bus around and took the track in the opposite direction much faster than Alison would have liked, as if he feared they might otherwise not reach civilisation again before dark. That had to be hours away, surely. She looked at her watch.

Yes, it was only a quarter till three. If they cut the animal sanctuary visit short, they might still arrive back in Corinbye less than an hour behind schedule. She'd get straight into a cool bath…

The sky looked weird—thickly clouded and bluish-black, as if a storm was approaching, even though Alison couldn't imagine that rain was in the air, with this oppressive dry heat. The mini-bus had air-conditioning, but it was no match for today's conditions. Her thighs sweltered in a patch of scorching sun coming through the side windows.

Sam turned left and they seemed to be heading deeper into the mountains again—west, towards the fires. Was the animal sanctuary in this direction? He made another turn, and as they travelled along the side road he'd taken, Alison saw a Rural Fire Service tanker truck roaring along the route they'd just left, sending up a boiling trail of dust that streamed in their direction because of the wind.

She had absolutely no idea where they were, and she had a horrible suspicion that Sam didn't either.

'This is ridiculous!' Valda said, in the seat just in front, and for once Alison had to agree with the complaint.

'Shouldn't you look at the map again, young fella?' Eddie asked.

'I think we've gone off the map,' Sam admitted. 'I'm going to ask for directions in a minute.'

Ask who?

It was twenty past three now, and they seemed to have gone even deeper into the wild bush country than before. As they crossed a clearing, Alison saw the sky for the first time in some minutes, since it had been obscured by the thick, scrubby forest that lined their current—unknown—route.

And, oh, dear lord, it was lurid, orange and purple and black like a massive bruise, and towering overhead like the end of the world. She'd never seen anything like it in her life. Everyone gasped.

'I think I'm going to throw up,' Sarah said next to her. 'Can we stop?'

'I can see some farm buildings up ahead to the right,' Sam answered. 'Can you wait?'

'No.'

So he screeched to a halt and they lost another ten minutes while poor Sarah rushed off the side of the road into some dead grass and said goodbye to her lunch. Troy went after her with a towel and some water, then helped her back on board.

Sam roared off, found a mailbox—or rather a painted can nailed to a crooked post, reading 'RMB 4', that signalled the track leading to the farm he'd glimpsed through the trees. A short while later, they saw movement and people and a couple of vehicles, and Alison felt a wash of relief so strong that it left her legs shaking. She knew everyone else must be feeling the same.

The relief was short-lived.

Seeing their arrival, a man strode up to Sam at the driver's side window and gave a couple of short, impatient nods at his question. He was obviously keen to get back to the activity going on behind him, where two more men were doing something with flexible pipes and a pump.

'Directions?' Half his face was hidden beneath his battered hat. 'Yes, I can give you directions, but it's not going to do you much good.'

'Why not? I'm a competent—'

'Because we've just heard on the radio that they've closed the road. It's under immediate threat about ten kilometres south-west of here. Containment lines are broken, and if this wind keeps up they think the fire-front will come through our place tonight. It's out of control, we're on our own, and you're not going anywhere.'

CHAPTER FOUR

'THERE must be more than one road,' Valda said.

'That got closed this morning,' the man answered. 'Look, try the road back to Berringong if you want, it's no skin off my nose, but even the Fire Service in their big tankers had trouble getting through just now, they said on the radio. Paint was blistering on the vehicle.'

'Show me on the map,' Sam said. He looked pale and tense as he unfolded it. 'I'll have to phone the tour company.'

He started to pull a mobile phone from his pocket, but the farmer said tersely, 'You won't be in range for that out here. And we lost the land-line an hour ago. Power, too. We're on our own generator now.'

'Right.'

'If you stay, I can get a message through on the radio for the fire service to pass on, saying you're here and you're all OK.'

'Yes, because we'll have concerned relatives. And my boss.' Who was clearly going to kill him, as far as Sam was concerned. 'So show me…'

'Got a pen?'

'Here.'

'Well, you're off map for the first fifteen kilometres…'

The man described a couple of turns. Left after five k's at the big tree. Right on the far side of the creek. Or something. Alison didn't take it in.

'But here's where you go after that.' He made a jagged

line of blue along the route. 'Obviously, we'll make room for you here if you decide to stay put—'

'That's very generous of you, Mr...' Alison began, in chorus with a couple of similar comments from others.

'Steve,' he cut in. 'Steve Porter. Brother Richard and dad Frank, over there.' He gestured behind him. 'Jackie, my wife, is inside.'

'Very generous,' Alison repeated, letting go of a nightmare scenario in which they had to cower beneath the minibus while hell roared right over them. She couldn't see how they'd have survived. She couldn't begin to imagine what it would be like. And she had no desire to find out.

'There's no other town?' Sam asked.

'We're pretty isolated. And pretty busy right now. If you do stay, we'd appreciate some help.' Steve took a closer look at the occupants of the mini-bus, and his face fell. 'From those who can. Make your decision and let me know.'

He strode off, climbed into the battered four-wheel-drive truck parked nearby and started the engine.

'Guys?' Sam turned in the driver's seat. His lips were white. He looked about fourteen. 'I've stuffed up. And I can't take the responsibility of driving us back through a road that's been officially closed because of fire. We'll have to stay until it's safe to leave. Overnight, at least. Obviously, I have no authority over any of you in any way, but I do ask that you, um, try to do what these people want, be as useful as you can. This is one of those situations where...' He ran out of steam suddenly, and trailed off, before adding a whispered, 'I'm sorry.'

The four-wheel-drive truck veered past them, then rumbled over a metal grid that led into a fenced field where cattle grazed beneath scattered trees. The passenger door opened and a couple of reddish-brown dogs jumped out, then dogs and truck began to chase crazily all over the rough terrain, herding the brown and white cattle towards the far end of the field, where there was a gate.

Alison glimpsed the curve of a rocky stream-bed and guessed that this offered the animals their best chance of survival—some ground that was free of flammable vegetation and possibly a waterhole or two, although, from what she'd seen, most of the streams were almost dry. Shifting the beasts to this spot and opening any gates to give the animals freedom to run for their lives was all the farmers could do for them.

'We'd better introduce ourselves to the Porters,' Sam said.

'Right you are,' Eddie answered. He tried an efficient leap from the front passenger seat, but turned his ankle on the uneven ground and made a pained grimace as he massaged it.

No wonder Steve Porter's face had fallen as he'd surveyed his unexpected reinforcements. There was tiny Mrs Hiromichi in her pastel linen suit, with barely a word of English at her command, there were four senior citizens, one of whom laboured just to breathe, there was a corpulent man in his mid-fifties who'd probably just sprained his ankle...

And there's me, Alison realised. American tourist. No Australian bush skills at all. Grateful for a roof over my head. He probably thinks I'll treat his home like a hotel.

The other four—Sarah and Troy, Nico and Sam—just might be worth something. No, not Sarah, Alison revised at once. She'd stumbled out of the mini-bus and was now bent double with her body locked in violent heaving again, poor thing. She'd barely managed to eat or drink at lunch.

Everyone else climbed out of the vehicle, too.

'This is impossible, incompetent, absolutely disgraceful,' Valda complained.

Alison had gone beyond that attitude now. Her scalp tingled and she felt a surge of strange, determined energy.

'Yes, it is,' she said crisply. 'But that's not going to save our lives.' At the edge of her vision, she saw Nico glance sharply in her direction, but she didn't shift her focus. 'Sam's right. This is one of those situations where you do what has to be done, and keep the recriminations for later.'

'Yes, Sam, can we meet these people, thank them for taking us in and find out what they need from us?' Nico asked. 'They cannot afford for us to be a burden at a time like this.'

His air of confident, efficient yet laid-back authority captured everyone's attention at once, and Alison felt an overpowering flood of thankfulness that he was here. Whatever breakdown of personal trust and connection had happened between them seven years ago, she had never doubted him in a crisis and she didn't doubt him now. She had to suppress an almost painful longing to seek the refuge of his solid body against hers and for a moment her legs felt as if they might buckle beneath her.

'Sarah, Jerry,' he went on, 'you'll need to shelter in the house, or wherever the Porters feel is safest, and simply stay out of the way until the danger is past. Sam, Troy and myself should be of some use to the men.'

'And me,' Eddie said stoutly.

Nico nodded and was tactful enough not to argue. 'The rest of you…'

'Can cook,' Joan said, surprising everyone. 'I count fifteen people, and the men, especially, will need to be fed. They could be working all night. I'm not just going to sit around like a stuffed chook. And we'll look after the dogs, once they've been brought inside.'

'We should get all our gear out of the bus, too,' Deirdre added. 'Midori and I will do that. Come on, love, let's see if I can explain to you what's going on, because you're probably as frightened as we are and you don't have a clue.'

She put a comforting hand on the Japanese woman's shoulder, and while the rest of them walked over to Richard and Frank Porter, she mimed energetically, making lost-our-way-on-the-map gestures and whooshing fire noises and crouched, sheltering movements. Mrs Hiromichi nodded in reply, looking neat and polite and round-eyed. How much did she understand?

Walking towards the Porters, Niccolo observed his own state of mind with a level of detachment that he'd experienced before in the face of a looming crisis. Adrenalin would start to surge later, but for now he felt calm, alert to the nuances that were going on around him. It wasn't hard to see who would pull their weight and who wouldn't, although there might be the odd surprise in the mix.

He couldn't help looking at Alison more than at anyone else. With her naturally pale skin, she looked whiter and more frightened than anyone, and he wanted to tell her, *Have some trust. In yourself, and in the rest of us. I know your track record in an emergency. You're afraid you'll let somebody down, but you won't. You've always been a lot stronger than you know, in so many ways.*

He started moving in her direction, ready to say it, but now didn't seem like the right time. He saw her push strands of her flaming hair back from her forehead with that deceptively fine-boned and fine-skinned hand, and her neat white teeth scraped across her beautifully moulded lower lip, making him remember the lush gift of her kiss.

'We weren't expecting visitors,' Frank Porter drawled when the group reached him. He was a weatherbeaten-looking man somewhere in his fifties, with gnarled hands, rolled-up sleeves and an aura of laconic intelligence and strength. 'Any of you been through anything like this before?'

'I have.' Again, it was Joan who spoke, surprising them with her matter-of-fact attitude. 'Fifty years ago, on my brother's farm in South Australia. Not as extreme as this, but we had to beat out the flames around the house with wet hessian sacks.'

Frank looked doubtful as to whether this experience would count for much now, Alison noted. Joan wasn't in her twenties any more.

'Don't worry,' the elderly woman said to her new host, eyeing the diesel-powered water pump he was setting up. 'I'm not proposing to man a hose, but I'll help your wife in the house. She's filling the bathtub and sinks, wetting blankets and towels?'

'Yes.' He looked at the group again. 'Some of you are going to need clothes. We'll fix you up. And we've got plenty of food.'

He sketched out what they could expect the rest of the day to bring, using short, uncompromising phrases that made Alison's stomach start to churn harder than ever.

An attack of raining embers would come in advance of the fire itself. In these conditions, spot fires could start a mile or more ahead of the wall of flames. This was a crown fire, raging through the treetops with intense heat as the volatile eucalyptus oil erupted into the air, passing within a few minutes.

Fire was unpredictable at the best of times. They might get lucky, but they shouldn't count on it. If the crown fire did come through, they'd have the pump working at full force during this mercifully short phase, flooding the roof and the sides of the house with water.

Even after it had passed, however, the danger wouldn't be over. The ember attack in its wake could last for hours.

The vigil against treacherous sparks setting flammable material alight on or around the house would probably continue all night, even if the wind dropped.

With the time they'd had to prepare, property protected this way during a fire had a ninety per cent chance of being saved, he said. If the place was unattended, it would have a ninety per cent chance of being lost. He didn't mention the odds of human survival.

While listening to this bald, dramatic summary, Alison looked around. Her hair had dried after the swim earlier, and the wild wind had gradually pulled strands of it free from the high ponytail she'd made. They whipped around her face, getting in the way of her vision, tangling into fine, tight knots and adding to the eerie, unpleasant sense of atmosphere that oppressed her as she took in what she saw.

The ground immediately surrounding the house was relatively clear of vegetation, to a distance of about a hundred and fifty feet, she estimated, but there were some wooden outbuildings, a stand of gnarled old fruit trees and a couple of lines of fence.

Any of those things could catch fire in these conditions, especially given the wall of forest to the west, beyond the cleared ground. Behind the wall, that bizarre, terrifying sky still loomed, more garish than ever.

The house itself looked like a typical farm dwelling. Part of it was obviously quite old. The walls and the enormous fireplace and chimney at the side were made of stone, but the rafters in the roof must be wooden ones, beneath a red-painted metal roof with wavy undulations in it that were shaped like a crinkle-cut potato chip. There was a wooden veranda as well.

Connected to this original building by a second veranda—concrete-floored and screened in with wire mesh—was a newer place made of reddish brick. Newer, but not new.

Nineteen-forties, maybe? A little older? Alison knew next to nothing about Australian heritage architecture. It had wooden window-frames and yet another veranda, also with a floor of wooden planking, wooden supporting posts and a rather attractively curved roof made of that same crinkly painted metal.

Beyond the house to the east was the field—no, Sam had used the word 'paddock' today—where the cattle had recently been grazing, and there were more paddocks to the south and south-west of the house as well.

There seemed to be almost no grass left on the ground for the cattle to forage, but the scattered eucalyptus trees which gave the animals summer shade would erupt like torches when the fire-front came through, Frank had said.

In a near corner of the east paddock, a pond had been bulldozed for water storage, but the level was well below the top of the eroded earthen bank and the water looked as muddy as milky tea. She saw Richard Porter unrolling a thick white length of flexible plastic pipe towards the pond.

It wasn't going to reach.

No, OK, he had another length of it, and some kind of coupling.

She assumed the cold water flowing through it would be enough to keep the plastic from melting in the radiant heat, until she heard Frank say, 'As soon as we've got you kitted up, Niccolo, Sam, Eddie and Troy, I'm sticking shovels in your hands and you're burying that pipe.'

'Where should I station the bus?' Sam asked.

'In the lee of the machinery shed.' Frank gestured beyond the house and Alison saw another very old building with stone walls on three sides and a tractor inside. 'We're putting our vehicles there, too.'

He led the way towards the house, and Alison saw two horses tethered to the veranda posts. Deirdre and Midori caught up to them, their arms full of handbags and back-packs. They'd have to go back for a second load, including the remnants of lunch. No one had drunk the champagne, and it remained unopened. Maybe the Porters might appreciate it tomorrow, Alison thought wryly. She devoutly hoped they'd all have a victory to celebrate.

She stepped onto the veranda of the newer house and found that Nico was beside her. Their eyes met and held, and he was close enough that she could feel his body heat, even against the competing heat of the scorching air. He cupped a hand around the curve of her waist, leaned towards her and murmured in her ear, 'Strange, isn't it? We're on a level playing field again, just the way we were when we first met.'

'Oh.' Her insides crumbled like melting chocolate. He still smelt the same as she remembered—soapy and warm and male—and her brain was as helpless as her body in its reaction to his nearness. She was shocked at how familiar he was to her senses after so long. 'What do you mean, a level playing field?'

'We're both foreigners. Highly competent in certain areas, plenty of crisis situations under our belts, but we know nothing about an emergency of this particular kind.' His mouth hardly moved as he spoke. This was for her alone. 'We're going to be stretched to breaking point tonight, the way we were sometimes during our internship, and nothing in our very different previous life experiences can truly help.'

She couldn't answer. She could only nod.

Her eyes were still locked with his, half-drowned in their jade and topaz depths. Narrowed as they were in the harsh light, she could see the evidence of the years that had passed. He had lines there now. Just faint ones. The kind you wanted to kiss before you made a trail of imprints with your lips all the way down to his gorgeously shaped mouth.

She was astonished that she still felt this pull towards him. And she was even more astonished when something in his face changed and she was sure that she glimpsed an answering awareness.

'If it helps,' he added, 'I'm very glad that you're here.'

'Are you?' she managed breathlessly. 'Yes, me, too. I never wanted to—' But, no, she couldn't say any of that. Not now. 'Me, too,' she repeated, and didn't care how much her face and her voice and the softness of her body gave away.

'You usually had an exceptionally cool head in a medical crisis,' he said, exceptionally cool himself. 'Once it was actually in progress. It seemed to astonish you every time, but it never astonished me.'

That? That was why he was glad?

She'd just imagined the rest.

'You had a cool head, too,' she got out thinly, just as they reached the comparative coolness of the house, behind Frank, Joan and Sam. 'You were an excellent doctor.'

'Hi,' said a woman, coming out of the kitchen at the end of the corridor.

'Load of lost tourists,' Frank told her.

'I saw the mini-bus. Had a small hope that it was a fire crew, but then I looked out of the window, and—' She stopped. 'I've put the kettle on.'

'No time for that now,' her father-in-law told her, over a moan from Valda. 'I'm going to get this lot organised. Able-bodied ones outside, a couple of them on kitchen duty with you and the rest wherever we can put them.'

'Yes, all right.' Jackie's voice remained clipped but cheerful.

'Sam, Troy, Nico, Eddie, follow me and we'll ransack

Steve's wardrobe and drawers. Going to be an iffy fit on some of you.'

The five of them disappeared in the direction of the bedrooms, while the others continued to mill around outside the kitchen door. The corridor was dim after the brighter light outside, and it took all of them a few moments to adjust their vision. When Alison did, she was shocked at what she saw.

Dark-haired, neatly built Jackie was *very* pregnant.

Why on earth was she still here?

'OK, so who're my kitchen staff?' Jackie asked, ignoring the shocked stares that everyone was giving her by this time.

'Deirdre and I,' Joan said.

Valda sniffed and stayed silent. They could all hear Jerry's harsh breathing as he stood next to her.

'Me, I suppose,' Alison added, 'although I'd be happy to help outside, Jackie, if you could find me the right clothes.'

Shorts and a crop top had seemed sensible this morning, but they didn't now. They seemed about as sensible as a heavily pregnant woman hanging about waiting for a bush-fire to arrive.

'Yes, you look about my size,' Jackie said. 'My usual size,' she corrected herself.

'And I'm a doctor.'

'Not an obstetrician, I don't suppose? A rural GP?'

'No. You're not…?'

'No.' She met Alison's close scrutiny with a steady face, while everyone else looked on. 'I'm not in labour.'

'When is the baby due?'

'Three days ago. It is not coming before Monday, however. It has been told.'

'I'm pregnant, too,' Sarah came in quietly. She still looked pale and washed out. 'Nine weeks.'

Alison didn't know whether to find Jackie's firm tone reassuring or very scary. 'Why are you still here?' she said.

'Because there was no big neon sign overhead, telling me to go.' Jackie sounded frustrated and angry. 'It's only just over an hour to the hospital, and this is my first baby, so it'll probably be slow. I'm country born and bred, I wasn't going to panic and camp out in town for weeks in advance. I've had a textbook pregnancy all the way through. And these are once-in-a-hundred-years conditions, if you haven't realised. The fire danger index is off the top of the scale. Even this morning, we had good reason to think it would be days, if ever, before the fire-front reached us from the west. Containment lines had held.'

'They're broken now, Frank told us,' Joan said.

'Yes,' Jackie acknowledged tersely, then continued, 'He and Rich got here last night to help us. Steve wanted to bulldoze a fire-break west of our biggest paddock to protect the stock, just in case. We knew that local fire crews were out in force, with more coming in from Victoria and other parts of the state. And we decided that, yes, I should go today, in case some lunatic criminal arsonist started a new blaze closer by, but we still thought we had plenty of time.'

She paused for a moment to take an extra deep breath. No one else moved or spoke. Her fierce attitude dared them to question the decisions she and her family had made.

'We did some fire readiness work around the place,' she continued, 'and I packed my bag at lunchtime, ready to head down to my sister in Cooma, then we tuned into the Fire Service frequency on the two-way radio and heard the news about the fire jumping the road and threatening two of the crews. We saw the sky, heard how fast the fire was moving in these awful conditions and realised I'd have to stay put. Just like the baby's going to stay put, until the road is open again.'

She sounded so implacable about it that Alison decided—almost—to believe her. Obstetrics seriously wasn't her area, but maybe wishful thinking as strenuous as Jackie's could reap the desired result. A lot of first babies came late.

'Right, clothes,' Jackie muttered as she lumbered down the corridor. 'For all of you, even if you're not planning on getting out there with a hose, because the radiant heat if the fire-front hits…' She didn't finish.

They were all kitted out in ten minutes. Natural fibres, not synthetics, wool for preference. Long trousers and long sleeves, thick to provide maximum protection. Work boots and work gloves for those who were going outside. Hats, preferably wool or felt.

On Eddie and Jerry, nothing really fitted or fastened adequately, and Midori was almost swimming inside Jackie's snuggest polo neck and jeans. Alison wore a pair of Jackie's black wool trousers, with a long-sleeved yellow cotton blouse on top and a wool sweater put aside to add later, especially if she went outside.

Nico looked like an Italian prince masquerading as a peasant in scuffed rubber boots, ancient jeans and a hand-knitted and home-spun wool sweater made of natural black sheep's wool. The wool wasn't really black, the way his eyes weren't really brown. It was an uneven dark chocolate colour, with a dash of pepper, and it was too long in the sleeves and too short at the waist. His white T-shirt stuck out at the bottom.

He looked a little amused about it, but at the same time very determined and square-jawed because he was under no illusions. This wasn't a game.

The 'able-bodied men' disappeared out into the worsening conditions, and Jackie, Joan and Deirdre got their heads together about the catering. Valda took Jerry off into a corner of the living room, where the curtains had been dragged back behind the walls, rolled up and fastened tight with masking tape.

Valda was worse than useless, Alison thought angrily—until she saw the anxiety that was screwing up the older woman's face and realised how genuinely worried she was.

And I'm a doctor, she thought. That's what I need to focus on.

She should find out what medical supplies the Porters had on hand, whether there was a first-aid kit in the mini-bus, and whether Nico had any useful Conti pharmaceuticals in that leather backpack of his. She should ask Jerry some searching questions, give him the best chest exam she could without a stethoscope, and make sure he was as adequately medicated as possible, in advance of breathing conditions that could well get a lot worse.

A quiet word with some of the others about their health status would be a sensible precaution also. Any asthmatics in the group? Any significant pre-existing medical conditions of any kind—less obvious, say, than a pregnancy at forty-plus weeks gestation?

What about Sarah? Was she at risk in any way, or merely miserable? Dehydration could be a problem if she couldn't keep enough food and fluid down, and nerves must be making her morning sickness worse. Alison had to fight not to feel queasy herself. Like all of them, she was facing the serious possibility that this could be the worst night of her life.

And Eddie? He'd been limping after the jaunty leap from the mini-bus. His weight and lack of fitness coupled with a significant sprain wouldn't make him an effective worker and could predispose him to further more serious injury. She wondered if he would realise that himself, or if she should try and persuade him to join the women and children—unborn—inside.

She'd give him half an hour to get sensible, she decided, then confront him with some blunt questions. She couldn't afford to worry about his hurt feelings at a time like this.

Going into the kitchen, she heard the tail end of Jackie's summary of the precautions they'd already taken, and those they still needed to make.

'And the downpipes are blocked and the gutters filled with water. The dam is very low, but Steve thinks there's enough water in it to pump continuously for an hour, as long as they can get the pipe buried in time. We'll keep the tank water for household use, as well as for running the smaller hoses and keeping blankets wet. The generator's pretty vulnerable. If it goes and we don't have power, we have torches, candles, a gas camping stove and lights.'

'Do you have a first-aid kit, Jackie?' Alison asked.

'Yes, we do. It's pretty basic, though.' In an aside, she added, 'Flour's in a bin in the laundry, Joan.'

Midori and Deirdre were cutting up fruit, and Joan seemed to be mixing something in a big bowl. Jackie herself was cutting garlic and onions on a big wooden chopping board, with a plastic bag of minced beef and several cans of tomatoes on the bench in front of her.

'Any other medical supplies in the house?' Alison went on. 'Could I check your bathroom cabinet? I'd like to know where we stand, get things organised and easily to hand, in case of any emergency.'

She could envisage a raft of them. Burns, smoke inhalation, gashes and sprains. Some she didn't even want to consider. Snake bites? Animal attacks? What happened if fear-crazed wildlife sought shelter at the house? Or had she gone into movie-land now?

'Oh, yes, that would be great,' Jackie said, wiping her sleeves across eyes streaming from onion fumes. 'Of course. My mother had asthma—she, uh, died a few years ago.' She sounded as if her grief was still fresh. 'But we still have a nebuliser and some of the medicines she had to take. I don't know if—Take a look. Put together whatever you can find that you think we might want.'

Alison spent fifteen minutes ransacking the bathroom and the laundry for supplies. She consulted with Jackie again, and they decided that the best place for them was the spacious, old-fashioned bathroom's wide tiled bench-top. The room was apparently a solid box of brick and cement, and most of them might have to seek refuge in it as the fire came through. It could be a first-aid station and shelter in one.

'What are you cooking?' she asked the pregnant woman. 'It's starting to smell fabulous.'

'Meat sauce for spaghetti. Easy to serve in shifts and easy to eat with a fork while standing up. Who knows when we'll get the chance to have it?' she added in a tight tone.

'Which is why we're making a big plate of fruit, and pikelets with butter and jam,' Joan said.

Her cheeks were pink, and she and Deirdre both looked as if they were almost enjoying themselves. They were wiry women, uncompromisingly grey-haired, and they'd probably worked hard and with good cheer all their lives. Midori chopped her fruit neatly and silently, but she was clearly just as glad as the others to have something useful to do.

Valda had never discovered that particular secret to happiness. She sat on a couch in the living room next to her husband, alternately patting his hand or his shoulder in concern, and grumbling at him about not telling her the truth as to how he felt and not bringing all of his medication.

'Can I ask you a couple of questions, Jerry, and make sure you're as comfortable as we can get you?' Alison asked, and received a grudging assent.

He was already sitting upright in an armchair, his back

padded with cushions, and that would be the best position for him. Alison could see that he was short of breath, and that his respiratory rate was higher than it should have been at around twenty-two breaths a minute, as a rough estimate. His colour looked all right, though, no blue tinge to his lips or nail-beds.

'You have your inhaler, don't you?' she asked.

'Don't need it.'

'You do, Jerry! He hasn't remembered to take his blood-pressure medicine *or* his diuretic since we left home, even though I've reminded him a hundred times,' Valda added.

'How can I take that when we're going on tour buses every second day, Valda? You want me putting my hand up for a rest stop every ten minutes?'

'As if it would be—' Valda began impatiently.

Alison took a deep breath and cut across the bickering. 'Can I get you to use your inhaler now, Jerry?'

He shrugged. 'Might as well.'

She watched his technique and saw that it wasn't particularly effective, but realised that now wasn't the time for a lesson. Later, maybe. Or just keep in the back of her mind that he was only receiving about half the benefit from each dose that he should. He didn't seem frightened, just grumpy and resistant to help, so she was speaking as much to Valda as to Jerry himself when she said, 'Please, tell me the moment you have any concerns or needs. Rest is the best thing for you right now, and you're doing fine.'

Outside, the men were hard at work. Richard and Frank had the pumping system fully in place now, and were warming up the diesel-fuelled engine. Steve was operating the bulldozer, pushing a heap of firewood away from the house.

Logs splintered against the big metal blade, dust churned into the air and Alison wondered if the task was really worth doing, with all the other potential fuel around the place. She fully understood his inability to be idle, though. She'd have gone crazy herself with nothing to do. The sense of imminent doom in the air was tangible—the heat, the wind, the smell of fresh burning.

Sam, Troy and Eddie dug their shovels into the long mound of dry earth that Nico loosened ahead of them with a metal pick. His whole body moved with magnificent grace, and he'd temporarily discarded the wool sweater in the heat. When he raised the pick above his head, his T-shirt lifted to show an olive-skinned stomach that was flat and hard with muscle, and each thudding strike into the earth was efficient and effective.

Alison had never seen him work with such primitive physicality before. His shoulders and arms rippled and hardened in a fluid pattern with each downstroke. It was brute manual labour, way beneath the dignity—and beyond the ability!—of many doctors, let alone a Conti heir, and yet he did it with a raw male energy and power that stirred something deep and pulsing and yearning inside her.

In fact, she *had* seen him use his body in a similar way before, she realised. Or rather she'd felt it, rippling and rhythmic and thrusting, against her own eager heat. He'd felt so perfect and right and important in her arms, skin to skin. Her breath caught at the memory—her fingers and her stomach and her nerve-endings and her tingling breasts remembered, too—and she struggled to tear her gaze away and hold her racing pulses in check.

Eddie. She was here to check on Eddie, and then hunt up the first-aid kit in the mini-bus if he still seemed OK.

He didn't.

He was struggling, his work so slow and ineffectual as to be almost useless. Alison could see he was favouring the ankle he'd turned earlier. Time to tell him to stop.

'How about you come inside and take a break, Eddie?' she said, laying a hand on his arm.

He didn't even argue, just nodded and dropped the shovel in the dirt. His face was dark red and streaming with sweat, and her heart gave a thump of intuitive dread.

'Are you having any pain?' she asked. 'Chest pain?'

'Can't seem to get my breath. Feeling a bit crook.'

'Come inside,' she repeated, her mind racing. This surely wasn't a heart attack. The pain would typically be intense if it was. But there were other potential dangers. Stroke. Serious dehydration. As long as she could keep him calm and quiet…

She could see that Nico had halted his rhythm and was watching them, assessing the older man's poor condition, and she knew he'd be plotting out the same scenarios that she was.

Her gaze locked with his, but she couldn't ask him right now about what medicines he had in his day-pack, let alone do what she really wanted and bury herself in his arms, seeking a lost piece of paradise from long ago. She had to get Eddie into the house.

He leaned heavily on her shoulder the whole way and didn't speak, and she knew she'd want to make frequent checks on him even if he spent the rest of the day lying down. 'Glass of water, bit of a break and I'll be fine,' he finally said, just as they entered the house. She didn't believe him.

She found a room and a bed, and that was all she cared about right now. Eddie was happy to lie down. She felt his pulse and counted ninety-five beats a minute. Too fast, but not dangerously so. She wouldn't have been surprised to find it higher. It seemed reassuringly regular, with a good volume. His breathing rate was around twenty-four.

'Can you tell me about your medical history, Eddie?' she

asked. 'Any history of heart trouble or breathing problems? What's your blood pressure like, do you know?'

'Well, my doctor has me on something for it, so it's come down from what it was a year or two ago.'

'What was it then?'

'One-sixty over a hundred. No heart trouble, though.'

'But it's come down since, and you've been taking the medication?'

He nodded.

'You have it with you?'

Another nod.

She'd check what it was and see if it was the same as Jerry's. If so, the latter could borrow a dose.

'I'm just going to leave you resting, then, Eddie. No more hero stuff, though, OK? It'll backfire and we won't thank you for it!' She softened the statement with a grin, and he smiled back.

'Tea's up,' Jackie said, when Alison entered the kitchen to report that she'd put Eddie on a bed in what looked like a spare room.

'I'll take him a big mug, milky and sweet,' Joan said.

'Water, too, Joan, if you could,' Alison told her. 'It's like a blast furnace out there. They'll all be losing a lot of fluid.'

'Could you let the men know about the tea, Alison?' Jackie said.

'I'm not sure that they'll want to stop.'

'They're stopping,' she replied shortly. 'It's probably their last chance.'

So Alison went back out, just in time to see the first blackened leaves beginning to fall. They were harmless, as far as she could tell—just fragments of bark and leaf, pungent and scorched.

She saw Frank rubbing a couple of them to powder in his fingers as he looked up at the hellish sky. He had a wary, calculating look on his face, and she knew he was probably comparing today's conditions with those he'd experienced in the past.

More dangerous? Less?

What would happen if the wind changed?

'Come eat,' she told the men. 'Jackie's insisting.'

They nodded and downed tools, heading at once for the house. The job was nearly finished. Alison caught up to Nico and touched his dusty arm.

'What drugs and equipment do you have in your day-pack?' she asked quietly.

'Not much. The new Conti NSAID—in case I get a head-ache! Samples of our new inhaler. A couple of first-aid items that must be in the mini-bus kit as well. That's about it.'

'Even if it's not much, could you unload it in the bath-room, where I'm setting up? Maybe I'm making too much of this—maybe it's just the conditions that are spooking me—but I could see us ending up like a military casualty station here. I'm going to get the first-aid kit out of the mini-bus, too.'

'I'll come with you.' He veered in an unexpected direc-tion and they collided, his upper arm hard against her shoul-der, where it left a smudge of dust. 'Sorry.' He frowned and tried to brush the dust away, but his fingers were just as dirty, and damp as well. The mark stayed. 'Sam's moved it, see?'

She followed his gesture and saw the mini-bus next to the other vehicles, behind the shed some metres from the house. 'I didn't even notice.' She shook her head, annoyed at herself.

'Other things on your mind.'

Him, at this moment, but she didn't want him to know that. 'Just a few,' she drawled.

He didn't answer, because somehow he didn't need to. She knew their thoughts were both travelling along the same track—or ricocheting wildly inside the same box, more like.

They reached the mini-bus, which Sam hadn't bothered to lock. 'I should have asked him where the kit was,' Alison said, but Nico located it almost immediately, in a pull-out tray beneath the front passenger seat. It didn't look big enough to contain many of the items she'd been hoping for. Plastic airways, protective eye pads and gel burn dressings, for example.

Nico didn't seem satisfied either. 'Let's check elsewhere.' He stretched his body into the vehicle again. Standing just behind him, Alison watched the way the muscles in his back moved, and the way the fabric of Steve's faded jeans hugged the shape of his thighs. She closed her eyes.

Don't do this to yourself, Alison.

'There might be something else,' Nico muttered.

And in the glove compartment he found some rolls of sterile gauze and a packet of acetaminophen tablets. Paracetamol, they called it here. Not exactly life-saving medical technology, but worth bringing into the house all the same.

He slammed the door shut, while Alison stood there with the kit in her hands, stupidly slow to move. She felt drained of strength and purpose suddenly, after the way her mind had been racing and planning for the past hour.

Hugging her arms around her body, she watched another blackened leaf twirling towards the ground as if it had mesmerised her. Raking her teeth hard across her dropped lower lip, she felt only the slightest sensation even though she knew she'd already abraded them this way many times.

She didn't realise how closely Nico was looking at her until he spoke—or how close to each other they were standing. 'Something else we ought to get taken care of before we go back to the house, I think,' he said softly. 'We've been thinking about it, haven't we? Not sure if it's business or pleasure, and I'm not sure when we'll get another chance, but there's only one way to deal with this.'

'With what, Nico?'

'Curiosity? No, it's more than that, but I don't have a name for it. I just want to get rid of it. Understand it. Understand you, and what you do to me, and how it is possible that you still can, after so long.'

The words startled her, and her gaze jumped to his face. Lord, he was going to kiss her. He was. His eyes were fixed on her mouth. And they both knew she wouldn't turn her face away.

Curiosity? She didn't have a better name for it either, although she knew the word he'd used was wrong. Curiosity was for cats. This emotion was way more powerful than that, surging over her like a wave, making her eyes prick with tears.

But then a door slammed over at the house, and even though Nico didn't look towards the sound, she could see the change in his intent. 'You have a burnt leaf in your hair,' he said.

'Oh, I do? Well, of course I do, they're falling like black snow now.'

'Yes, I expect we'll all get a lot dirtier than this soon, but for the moment…' He didn't finish the sentence, just reached out and threaded the leaf free, then held it out to her.

'It's ominous,' she said. 'Nico, I'm…scared.'

Her skin sizzled with it, and her heart jumped. The adrenalin was too close to the sensation of female awareness. The two feelings tangled together inside her and she couldn't keep them apart. She wished he had kissed her, and had to hold herself back from touching him—his hair, his strong male jaw, the sturdy bone of his shoulder.

'You're too sensible not to be scared,' he agreed.

'Then you are, too?'

He gave a wry smile. 'The adrenalin is starting to flow now, yes.' They still stood very close to each other, their legs almost touching.

'I don't want it to happen.' She didn't care how weak it sounded. She couldn't have hidden anything from him right now. Not her fear, not her awareness, not her relief that he was with her. 'I don't want to be here. I want a reprieve. If the wind drops or veers…'

She was practically begging him to take her in his arms, doing everything except saying the words, but maybe those sorts of signals didn't get through at a time like this. Maybe the adrenalin was confusing him, too.

'We can't hide behind those hopes,' he said. 'We can't…let this get out of control.'

'No.'

'I'm thinking of soldiers about to go into battle, or surgeons before a ground-breaking operation, wondering if this is anything like how they feel. The smoke smells fresher, doesn't it?'

'I wish we could see beyond the trees.'

'Let's get back to the house.' He began to stride in that direction immediately.

'OK. Yes. You're right. We must.'

Half an hour later, they saw the first live embers begin to fall.

CHAPTER FIVE

NICCOLO felt rather than saw the change in the atmosphere. He wasn't allowing himself the luxury of time to stare at the lurid sky right now. But the heat had intensified and the smoke smelt so fresh it was like standing in front of a bonfire and personally feeding the flames.

He'd never been a tea drinker, but as he'd milled around in the kitchen with some of the others, gulping in the sweet, strong, milky brew while it was still piping hot, he'd begun to understand why Joan had urged it on him. The drink had soothed him, made him sweat and refreshed him to a surprising extent.

He hadn't spent long outside, just long enough to see a change in the way Steve and his brother and father were working. The defensive work was over and the battle had begun as they patrolled for the tiny sparks which would have no trouble igniting fuel in this intense heat and wind and dryness. He would join them again as soon as he'd satisfied himself as a doctor that he'd done what he could for the less able-bodied people inside.

He took a quick look at Jerry and Eddie, confirming Alison's sense that if they stayed quiet and sensible and kept up a good intake of fluids their health wasn't of urgent concern. Jerry had a dose of Eddie's blood-pressure medication ready to take at his usual time, with the evening meal.

Nico kept getting flashes of memory about the year he'd spent in Sierra Leone at a time when he'd still felt wounded and confused over the sour end to Alison's trip to Italy, questioning her behaviour, his father's attitude and his own response. Who had really been at fault? All of them, perhaps.

He'd thrown himself into the life-saving work of medicine in the developing world, had almost needed the primitive conditions in a strange way. He'd pushed himself harder than he ever had in his life and had lived on adrenalin and comradeship and his patients' smiles.

Would today be anything like that? How well equipped was he for heroism these days? Would Alison be a help or a dangerous distraction?

Alison didn't know, at first, that the black snow had turned to living orange.

She was inside the house, trying to do something for Sarah in impossible conditions. At her hospital in Ohio, she would have whipped in an IV line in a heartbeat—or even more likely asked a junior member of staff to do it for her—in order to push in around 200 ml per hour of normal saline and get Sarah's systolic blood pressure up.

She couldn't believe how quickly the lack of basic equipment turned a simple case of threatened dehydration into a potentially life-threatening medical emergency. She was shocked at how it panicked her, too. She felt stripped of her expertise, vulnerable, a fraud. Was she a doctor at all, when she didn't have machines to measure things and colleagues to consult with and the authority of a white coat and an official name badge?

Sarah couldn't keep anything down. She'd tried tea, juice, a sweet lemon drink and plain water. She'd tried the little buttered pancakes that Joan called pikelets, crackers, salted potato chips and seedless grapes. But her empty, churned-up, nervous stomach rebelled every time, and in these conditions she just couldn't afford to go for too long without fluids.

She'd almost fainted when she'd stood up from her chair in the kitchen, and her pulse was weak and rapid. Her eyes looked sunken and her skin less taut than it should be. Alison had gently pinched her forehead and the action had left a brief 'tenting' effect when the skin should have flattened out again at once.

In desperation, Alison set her up in the bathtub, of all places, making it comfortable with cushions and a padded quilt. The bathroom was the coolest and safest room in the house at least. Sarah could lie down, and she wouldn't have to move.

'Try to relax,' Alison told her new patient, her own limbs as tight as stretched elastic bands and her jaw actually shaking.

'Could you perhaps try to set me a better example?' Sarah retorted.

'I'm sorry. I know I'm asking the impossible.'

Sarah struggled to sit but swayed at once. Alison helped her as she bent over her bucket again, then reached for tissues and a damp facecloth. 'No, *I'm* sorry,' Sarah managed a minute or two later. 'You don't need to have me like this, and then getting snarky at you on top of it.'

She looked deathly pale, and she was slightly built, nothing in reserve. Nico, appearing in the doorway, looked like a giant by comparison. Alison felt a wash of relief just at the sight of him. Instinctively, she had an utter trust in his courage and good sense. He'd let her down once, behaved in a way she still didn't understand, but that had been personal while this was a crisis that affected other lives than just their own. He wouldn't let her down today.

She wanted to ask him about the conditions outside, but he didn't give her a chance.

'I've taken a follow-up look at Jerry and Eddie,' he reported to her, when she had moved to join him in the corridor just beyond the doorway.

'Thanks,' she answered.

The light here was dim and shadowy, and enveloped them in a greater sense of intimacy than she was used to in a professional setting. Where was the harsh fluorescent glare, bouncing off polished hospital floors and bland hospital walls? It distracted her to have to stand this close, and she couldn't see his face clearly. His eyes looked darker than usual, and his jaw even squarer and stronger.

'Still no real cause for concern, either of them,' Nico continued. 'I'm going to go back to the men outside.'

'So you haven't been out there since our teabreak?'

'Only for a minute.'

'How's it looking?'

'I'm not an expert.' His eyelids lowered briefly over his incredible eyes, shadowing them still more, and she knew he didn't want to say out loud that conditions were worse. 'Is there anything else you need here first?' he added.

'An IV? Bags of saline? A blood-pressure cuff? Airways, burn dressings, morphine, a stethoscope, oxygen?'

He raised his eyebrows in recognition of the fact that she may as well have asked for the moon. 'As a substitute for the IV and the saline at least, do you have any electrolyte replacement?' he suggested.

'I'm not sure.' She chastised herself mentally because she hadn't thought of it herself. Too busy lamenting what she couldn't have. American doctors were spoilt.

'Check the bathroom cabinet,' Nico suggested. 'Even the freezer. There's a kind intended for children that's packaged as a frozen treat. I'm not sure what the brand names are here. The powdered kind saved us hundreds of lives in Africa.'

'Africa?'

'Sierra Leone. I spent a year there with Médecins Sans
Frontières.' He saw her jaw begin to drop, and frowned.
'But, of course, I guess you didn't know that.' He sounded
prickly and impatient, as if she somehow should have read
his career résumé.

'Now's not the time to be filling each other in on—'
Alison began.

'No, of course it isn't,' he cut in. His body snapped to
attention, and she realised they'd been leaning closer as
they'd listened to each other. The noise of the wind outside
was getting louder. 'It's not the time for a whole lot of
things I'd like to get to eventually, when we can. If we can.'
He shrugged and turned his mouth down. 'But as to the
electrolyte solution, check the cabinet.'

'I'll ask Jackie, too.'

'And I will pass onto you something that I learned in
Sierra Leone, if you won't think I'm treading on your toes.'

'My toes, right now, are begging to be trodden on!'

He nodded briefly. 'So don't waste your energy wishing
for equipment and supplies you don't have and that you
can't get. Remember, in a lot of cases the best thing you
can do for a patient is just to be there. To be someone for
them to pin their faith to, someone who acts in a way that's
worthy of their faith. Sometimes that's all it takes, I've
found.'

'Thanks. Thanks, Nico.' A wash of relief and renewed
confidence ambushed her. Something snapped back into focus. Of course she could do this! Self-doubt had become a
reflex and a habit, and suddenly it was one she very much
wanted to break.

He smiled. 'I'll tell you about a couple of cases some
time.'

'I—I'd like to hear.'

'Let me have a talk to Sarah now.'

'Please. I obviously need to get a better handle on how to function in this kind of setting.' She pressed her lips together, felt her heartbeat steady and firm.

'You're doing fine, Alison.' In his light accent, her name had a lilting quality. 'As I suggested a minute ago, my advice wasn't meant as a put-down.'

'OK.' She gave a terse nod.

'Are you?' he asked. 'OK?'

'Yes. Thanks. I am.'

'Good.' He touched her neck.

The contact was so brief that it disappeared again before she'd fully felt it. She felt it afterwards, a tingle on her skin like the brush of a cat's tail, and instinctively she brought her own hand up to rest it on the same spot. Fortunately, Nico didn't see.

He went back into the bathroom bent towards the tub.

'Sarah, whatever we find for you, this is the most important thing you can do for us,' he said. 'This is what you need to focus on. Your job, and it's as vital as anything the others are doing outside.'

'Oh, really?' She made a doubtful face.

'Yes. Just sip the drink, take an hour to get it down, if you have to. Then try some plain water or diluted juice and see if the sip-by-sip approach works there, too. I can see you're beating yourself up because you're taking, not giving, but no one is blaming you for that.' His rolling accent cajoled and reassured.

Sarah nodded slowly, and a tiny amount of colour crept back into her face. 'Thanks, no, I'm sure they're not. I'll try to stay calmer. Hormones and nerves don't mix well.'

'Would you like Troy to come and sit with you?' Alison suggested.

'I'm not taking him away from where he's needed, but if he could just come and say hi occasionally.'

'I'll tell him,' Nico said.

Alison couldn't find any electrolyte solution in the bathroom cabinet, but she found Jackie in the kitchen.

'Look,' Jackie said, and following her gaze through the window Alison saw a burning twig rain onto the ground. Sam beat at it with a heavy wet blanket, because the leaf litter around it was already smouldering, then ran back in the opposite direction out of sight, yelling words they couldn't hear, to someone they couldn't see. 'I'm going out there.'

'No, Jackie.'

'I have to. This is our land, our place. We've put so much into it. I don't want our baby born homeless.'

Recognising that argument was futile, Alison asked, 'Do you have any electrolyte solution? Sarah needs it, if you do.'

'You mean those sachets you mix into a drink when someone has a stomach bug?'

'Yes, those.'

'In the pantry, I think. Let me look. It'll be pretty old…'

At the back of a crowded shelf, she found a small cardboard box with several sachets left in it. The expiry date had indeed come and gone, but the sachets seemed sealed and intact. They'd be fine.

'OK, I'm going,' Jackie said. She soaked a woollen hat and put it on, then dunked the sleeves of her knitted sweater as deep as they would go in a bucket of water and splashed herself all over, heedless of the puddles she left on the floor. The sweater strained across her bulge.

'Don't do anything—' Alison began.

'Stupid. No.'

Behind her, the screen door didn't close because the wind kept it pinned back against the house, where it continued to rattle and bump with a maddening rhythm. Out beyond the veranda, Steve appeared and thrust a gushing hose into Jackie's hand, yelling and pointing.

Alison mixed up a tall glass of the electrolyte replacement. It was orange-flavoured and smelled very artificial. She found ice in the freezer and added several cubes, because the chill would blunt the odd taste a little. Back in the bathroom, she found Troy, ruthlessly and blatantly lying to his wife.

'Going good out there. Frank and Rich and Steve have everything in hand. Wind's dropped a bit, I think. If it starts to blow the other way, the fire will burn back on itself and we'll have nothing to worry about. It won't reach us at all.'

'Really?' Sarah said, her face a little brighter.

'The authorities always panic people in these situations and ninety-nine times out of a hundred nothing happens. But I'd better…you know…get back. Don't want to look like I'm not pulling my weight.'

'Love you.'

'Love you, too. Really, really love you, Sar.'

'Don't say it like that.'

Because it made Troy sound as if he wasn't coming back, Alison knew.

'No, OK, I just wanted to say it, that's all. Drink your drink.' He gave a tight-faced look at Alison. 'This'll do the trick for her, won't it?'

'It'll really help.' If Sarah could keep it down.

'Back soon.'

He disappeared, and immediately Sarah said, 'You should go, too, Alison. I'm not going to keep one of the able-bodied people out of action. Maybe just send Joan or Deirdre to give me some company?'

'Let's see how you do on that drink first.'

Sarah sipped obediently. 'Well, it's horrible…'

But at least they could conclude several minutes later that

it seemed to be staying down, and the action of taking slow, careful sips had calmed Sarah considerably, as had the comparative peace and coolness of the bathroom.

'Go,' she told Alison again. 'Make sure Troy's not doing anything crazy. Come back and tell me, when you get a chance, how much he was lying to me about everything being fine out there.'

'Of course. But I'm sure it's not as bad as it feels…'

Alison left the bathroom to the sound of jet planes screaming overhead. Big ones, she decided, surprised. Commercial airliners or cargo planes. They must be flying very low, because they'd blocked off the sun so that it was almost like night.

What on earth—?

She raced outside, overwhelmed by a dark feeling of dread, not even thinking to check on the people still in the house. Or the dogs. Joan had said she would take care of the dogs…

There were no planes. It was the sound of the fire, coming down on them. Alison was as shocked as if they'd had no warning at all. Somehow she hadn't expected it to arrive like this. She'd expected to see it before she heard it, but the smoke was so thick—black in some directions, yellow in others, boiling and completely opaque almost everywhere—that the sound was the clearest warning.

And above all she'd expected more time.

How fast must it be travelling? It was like a living creature now—a host of them, roaring and screaming in anger and pain, the loudest thing she'd ever heard in her life. Except that at some point, for an interval, she stopped hearing it. Just stopped. Had no sense of the sound at all, because everything else overwhelmed her more.

She lost track of where everyone was, or where safety lay. It didn't occur to her to go back inside when she was so clearly needed here. Frank threw a sodden blanket at her, yelling something she couldn't hear. Battling hurricane-force wind, Steve turned on the pump and water began to cascade over the house, hissing into steam at several points. With the narrower hose from the rainwater tank, he kept the ground around the little pump engine wet and cool.

Somewhere close by, glass shattered. In the forest, trees exploded, cracking like heavy gunfire or human groans. A burning branch the diameter of a grown man's arm fell from the sky, along with a rain of smaller ash and flames. Alison saw fire ripple out of nowhere towards the veranda and she began to beat at it frantically with the blanket, which already felt heavy in her arms.

No. It didn't. She couldn't let herself get tired. Not yet.

The tongue of flame suffocated and died, and she turned to find the next danger.

Time ceased to have meaning, and the heat was intense, solid, alive. Figures ran back and forth. Sam. Rich. Troy. People yelled, but she couldn't hear or understand what they said. She wondered where Jackie was.

Inside? She surely had to have gone inside by now, for the baby's sake. This smoke was choking. It stung Alison's eyes, hurt inside her lungs and threatened to make her gag. She saw Frank with a wet tea towel over the lower half of his face like a surgical mask, and debated rushing inside to find one for herself.

Did the debate last three seconds or three minutes? She never resolved it or found a moment to leave, because the fire kept finding new ways to challenge her, erupting out of nothing, falling from the sky, flying like a magic carpet, blowing like snow. She saw a red plastic bucket of water on the ground begin to sag like hot wax before her eyes and realised it was melting.

Melting. That's why I feel as if I am.

She dropped her blanket into the steaming water before the water all disappeared since the bucket couldn't hold it any more. The wind seemed even wilder now, and she was distantly aware of moving white-orange light breaking through the boiling curtains of smoke, high up in the tree-tops.

Nico appeared and fought her for the blanket. She fought back. 'Go inside!' he yelled.

'No! I have to put out the spot fires.'

'Everyone is going inside. Steve has the horses on the back veranda. We're going inside *now*!' He dragged her by the blanket, which she'd forgotten to let go of, and they pushed through the dripping curtain of water falling from the sprinkler on the roof.

On the veranda, Nico stopped suddenly and she cannoned into him with the sodden, acrid-smelling, filthy blanket between them. 'I have to say this,' he yelled above the barrage of noise. His fingers gripped hers, chafing them hard before settling into an iron stillness. 'It's stupid, but I have to say it. I loved you seven years ago, Alison.'

'Then what went wrong? Why did you stop?'

'I never stopped. You—'

She couldn't hear. It was crazy. He was yelling urgent, vital words to her that she desperately wanted to understand and answer from the heart, only she couldn't hear. The water drumming on the metal roof of the veranda had become drowned beneath a noise overhead that was indescribable now—crackling and howling and hissing and roaring and screaming—and she just couldn't hear, or read the movements of a gorgeous mouth distorted by Nico's vain attempt to yell even louder. They both dropped the blanket and it slowly slid down between them—making their legs damp.

'I never stopped either,' she yelled back, even though she knew he wouldn't hear her any more clearly than she'd heard him. 'I loved you. It hurt so much, and I never understood why. Was it really just because I couldn't handle your family?'

He swore. She could work that much out.

In Italian, she thought, and had a weird, false moment of clarity when she tried to remember what Italians said when they swore.

Then he kissed her.

No warning.

No preamble.

Just a desperate, frustrated swoop in the direction of her mouth, which was somehow already waiting and wanting, and that didn't help matters, because it made Alison move at the wrong moment so that Nico's lips landed clumsy and warm and hard, more on her chin than on her mouth.

They soon corrected the mistake.

He took her face between his hands and found the place he wanted to be. She closed her eyes so that the noise would stop—strangely, it did, or it seemed to, the way it had seemed to stop when she'd been wielding the blanket—and she didn't think about the end of the world happening all around them, just thought about him. She couldn't say anything, because he wouldn't hear, so she had to tell him everything with their kiss.

I don't think I ever stopped loving you.

I've been so angry with you.

Angry that you stopped being the person I expected you to be.

I still am. Angry with you. Angry with myself. In love with you. A version of you. Is it real? It's in my bones.

I've been kidding myself for years that I was over it, that I'd grown and learned and changed and I would be able to see you again without feeling any of this, but I was so wrong.

I just want you, and I think that's wrong, and insane, doesn't make sense at all, and this had better be the best kiss ever, buddy, because you have a lot of work to do to get me to trust this, and a heck of a lot to prove.

His mouth tasted of smoke at first, then they kissed the taste away and he was sweet and familiar and delicious, like the tea they'd both drunk a while ago.

And he was hers.

Right.

It really didn't make sense. They were both just grabbing at this—grabbing at the taste of each other, the heat, the memories, the melting pleasure, the pure connection with another living human being, the utter importance of love and touch. It had to be the kind of illusion that happened when death stared you in the face. Illusions could be powerful things.

Kisses were very powerful. Nico's kiss had the power to stir her to tears, and she was already shaking like a leaf. His arms, wrapped tightly around her, were the only thing that kept her standing. His mouth was the only thing that kept her alive. His beating heart was her only hope. They both gasped for breath, tried to bury themselves in each other, couldn't get enough.

Alison slid her hands up under his clothing, needing the touch and texture of his skin—the intimacy of it, and the familiarity. He buried his face in her neck and kissed the hair and the sensitive skin just behind her ear. His arms were so tight around her that they hurt, and she needed the pain and hardness to prove that they were both still alive. She loved the slightened roughened feel of his jaw against the much softer skin of her cheek and her mouth.

The veranda vibrated beneath their feet suddenly, and they heard yelling. They broke apart.

'My God, you never made it inside!' Frank shouted.

Alison could hear him more clearly than she'd heard Nico a few minutes ago, but she didn't have time to work out why this should be so.

'Too soon, Dad,' Steve said.

'Got to get back out there. Put out the spot fires. See what's happened to the generator. This is when it really…'

Both men stomped in their booted feet through the puddles on the veranda steps and the roar of the fire drowned their words again, turning their urgent conversation into a couple of sentence fragments. Alison frowned. Something was missing. Something had changed since she and Nico had sought shelter here.

Oh.

The water wasn't pumping onto the roof any more. She had no idea when it had stopped, connected it with what Frank had said about the generator and realised there was a problem.

Sam burst through the door and onto the veranda. 'Dr Conti, Dr Lane.' He swore, his voice shaking. 'I thought— I was scared you hadn't—But you're OK.' He laughed, a staccato burst of sound that he probably didn't even hear. It came from hysteria more than amusement, or even relief.

'We have to get back out there,' Troy said. Rich was hard on his heels.

For the first time Alison looked beyond the veranda, dazed and stunned both by what she saw and at the fact that the fire-front had come through so fast. If she'd been tempted to consider that the danger was over with the passage of the blaze through the treetops overhead, however, she was soon cured of that. The fire hadn't finished with them yet.

The wind had already died considerably after its howling hurricane force as the fire-storm passed, and the smoke hung in a choking pall. Everywhere, there was heat and flame. In the forest to the west not a leaf remained and trees still flared. Breathing caused pain.

The stakes that had held up the tomato plants in the vegetable garden were reduced to heaps of wind-blown white ash. Fence-posts glowed orange. Bitter black smoke rose from a couple of old car tyres. The paint on the side of the concrete water tank blistered and fried. In the paddock just to the left of the house, even the pats of cow manure flamed like miniature bonfires.

And burning embers still fell from the sky. Alison heard them hiss in the water that lay around the house and realised that the barrier of protective wetness wouldn't last long in this heat.

'Look at it,' she said to Nico, and only then realised how tightly they were still holding each other.

She stood right in the curved, iron-hard crook of his arm with her cheek against his shoulder and one hand gripping a fistful of the damp home-spun sweater that must belong to Steve. Her other arm pressed across his back and she held his waist so tight it must hurt. He was chafing her upper arm, rubbing his chin over her knotted hair, letting his thigh support her legs.

She felt dazed yet on high alert, ready to laugh or cry or run or scream or keep going for hours longer. She couldn't have sat down, couldn't have strung together more than a couple of clumsy sentences in a row. A sob rose inside her and came out more like a hiccup.

'What'll stop it?' she said. 'That inferno? Seems like it'll go all the way to the sea.'

'No, there's a reservoir a few kilometres east of here,' Nico answered. 'Frank was telling me. Part of the hydro-electricity network.'

'So it'll burn down to the water.'

'Yes, but that's where it will stop. And there's better access for the crews. They'll be able to protect the infrastructure. I'm going to get to work with that blanket,' he added, and let her go so that he could bend down and pick it up.

She felt bereft and had to bite back a whimpering entreaty for him to stay, for him not to let her go.

Pull yourself together.

Yes. Yes. She was fine.

She took a breath that knifed all the way down her dry windpipe. 'I'll see what's happening inside.'

She found Jackie first, standing at the kitchen sink, coughing violently and trying to soothe her seared throat with a drink of water. A hunk of singed hair hung beside her cheek but Alison didn't think she even knew about it.

The three farm dogs—one black and white border collie and the two red-brown ones whose breed Alison didn't know—sat watching her with big, patient eyes. They might be concerned about their mistress…or they might be waiting for food, or work to do. They'd behaved impeccably, and had shown complete trust in their humans, as had the soaking wet horses still tethered to the far veranda.

'Are you burned?' Alison asked Jackie.

'No, I got inside in time. We were worried about you and the other—I'm sorry, I've forgotten his name.'

'Nico. We were on the veranda. But you've burnt your hair. Are you sure you're not burnt anywhere else?'

'Have I?' She felt her head, and found the singed section. 'Oh, it smells. Oh, it's horrible.'

'Run some water through it.'

'We've got no water. No running water,' she corrected herself. 'We filled a lot of jugs and containers. But the pump's not working. Steve thinks it's the generator. He's gone to check.'

'Is everyone OK? How's Sarah? And Jerry? Midori?

Valda? Oh, look, don't answer, because I want to take a look at them all anyhow. Jackie, you look very pale.'

'Feeling a bit crummy. I was a bit late going inside.'

A prickle of alarm crept its way up Alison's spine, the way tongues of flame had crept towards the house half a lifetime ago. 'What are your symptoms? Is your throat sore? Do you have a headache? Nausea?'

'Yep. Last two are spot on.'

She gave proof of one of them half a minute later, bending desperately over the sink just as Sarah had done several times that day, while Alison's mind was still racing. Burnt throat? If it swelled and compromised her breathing… And what about the lung tissue itself?

Jackie's skin colour wasn't great right now, and her nostrils were blackened with smoke. Alison took her pulse, checked her respiration, listened for stridor and wheezing in her breathing. Nothing that set off urgent alarm bells. Not yet, anyway.

'Rest, Jackie,' she urged the other woman. 'Drink lots of water, and rest. I need to check on Sarah and the others.'

Sarah was great.

'I'm fine. Don't waste any time on me, Alison. I'm just sipping away here, feeling much better. Calmer. I'm going to try eating something soon.'

'It's smoky in here.'

'It's smoky everywhere. It's not that bad.'

Jerry was feeling it, though. He struggled to breathe, and didn't bother to claim any more that there was nothing wrong with him. Alison decided it was time to hunt up the nebuliser that Jackie had talked about, and soon had it working. Valda was too frightened and exhausted to complain about anything right now. She sat beside Jerry in the smoke-hazed living room of the farmhouse, holding his hand while he breathed through the nebuliser's clear plastic mask. She looked limp, an empty shell, all the fight and irritability gone out of her.

Midori and Deirdre were wandering around the house, looking out of windows and pointing, gabbling to each other in two different languages as if it didn't matter in the slightest that the other one couldn't understand. They seemed light-headed. Relief? The edge of hysteria?

Eddie sat slumped in a nearby chair. 'Don't worry about me,' he croaked, and his colour looked all right, much better than it had outside earlier. As long as Alison could keep him rested and fed and—

Tea. They'd all want tea.

'I must get Joan and Deirdre to do their thing with the catering again, as soon as we've got a way to heat the water,' Alison muttered to herself, then heard the same burst of half-hysterical laughter that Sam had given a few minutes ago, clattering from her own mouth this time.

They did happen to have the odd few open fires around the place, didn't they? One of them might just do for heating a kettle of water. Heating that spaghetti sauce, too, only she didn't feel the slightest bit hungry. Her mouth tasted too strongly and bitterly of smoke.

Oh. Head and stomach didn't feel too good either.

But you're the doctor, not the patient. Get it right, Dr Lane. She chuckled again, absent-mindedly, as she went in search of that packet of painkillers from the van, to wash some down with a big glass of water.

One thing she was absolutely sure of, she couldn't afford to end up as a patient tonight.

CHAPTER SIX

OUTSIDE, dusk had come, thick and hazy and too early for this time of the year. The smoke was so dense in the west that it blocked the light and made the hour seem much later than it really was. True darkness must still be an hour away.

Alison saw Frank, Steve and Nico grouped around a heap of tortured black metal a hundred metres from the house and went towards them across the hot grey-black dirt. In places, the clumps of dry grass that had been burned down to the roots crunched beneath her feet like uncooked spaghetti. Clean air and most colours—green, purple, blue—seemed like realities from another world, and only theoretical possibilities in this one.

Her senses weren't working right. She'd gone deaf to the volume of noise right at the fire-storm's height, and now her eyes had forgotten what colour was like. Even her pain awareness was off-line. What was that stinging feeling on her lower left leg, at the back?

When she focused on it, it got stronger, so she paused and twisted around and discovered a jagged, blackened slash in the fabric of Jackie's trousers. Beyond it, on her skin, was a burn. She didn't investigate it very closely because it didn't seem relevant at the moment, other than as an explanation for the pain. She must have gotten it at some point while she'd been wielding that blanket, but she didn't know when or how. She'd deal with it later.

'This was the generator,' she guessed aloud, when she reached the men.

Nico flicked a glance at her and their eyes met and locked

together for a moment, communicating the shared memory of their kiss and those shouted, emotional words that neither of them had understood. Had they even meant anything?

They couldn't possibly be repeated or explained, Alison felt. They were like the fire-storm itself, overwhelming everything else and passing so fast that even a short while later you couldn't remember how you'd felt, couldn't relive the detail, couldn't believe it had been real.

'Was,' Steve agreed, in answer to her comment. 'Pump engine went, too. If it hadn't lasted as long as it did, I think we would have lost the house.' A glowing ember fell in front of him, giving a telling punctuation to his comment. He didn't say out loud that if the house had been lost, the people in it might have been, too. The house was still at risk, and the temperature must still be close to a hundred degrees. 'We lost the feed shed. We've got nothing for the horses. Or the cattle, if they've survived.'

The comment fell heavily on all of them.

Alison saw Rich patrolling for spot fires and glowing heaps of coals with the hose from the rain-water tank in his hand, while Sam and Troy used wet blankets. On the far side of the house, she caught sight of another figure, also with a blanket, and realised it was Joan. Unstoppable, bless her.

She was calling to them. 'Come and look at this!'

They tramped over. On the way, Alison glanced for the first time towards the galvanised-iron machinery shed, behind which the farm vehicles and the mini-buses had been placed in a bid for their protection. The mini-bus's white paint looked scorched and blistered but it appeared basically intact…until she saw the way all four of its tyres sagged against the ground.

Apart from one old tractor, however, every one of the farm vehicles was a blackened hulk. One of them, lying several metres from the others, must have actually exploded, and the shed itself lurched like a drunk, crumpled on one side almost to the ground. Parts of some vehicles still burned.

'Look!' Joan said again. 'Someone's lit the barbecue for us.'

And there within the constructed arrangement of stones, covered in a blackened and ancient metal grill, a thick old chunk of log was burning merrily as if it really had been lit for the purpose and was waiting for its chance to cook burgers and steaks for them all.

'Do we put it out?' Steve asked. For the first time, he sounded as helpless as Alison felt.

'No, we put a kettle on it,' Joan said. 'We could all do with a good cup of tea, don't you think?'

'Could we, what!' Frank said.

'In a minute, I might whip up scones and some apple crumble, too.' Joan beamed. The drama seemed to be energising her, the way it had all afternoon. Blackened blanket still in hand and moving like a much younger woman, she almost galloped towards the house in search of the kettle, like a kid on a camping trip who's excited about cooking outdoors.

Nico watched her with a frown on his face, then Troy ran towards them, yelling that the veranda between the old house and the newer one was on fire, and the atmosphere became charged with frantic energy again as the men battled to put it out before it could spread.

It was another hour before anyone got their tea. By this time it was really dark, with a thick, starless sky overhead. If nightfall hadn't marked the passage of time, Alison would have had no idea about it at all. It could equally have been midnight or late afternoon. The air was a little cooler, too, but probably still well into the eighties.

Tree stumps and fence-posts that had looked burnt out in the daylight now revealed a mass of hot orange coals still glowing in their hearts. In every direction, eyes of fire watched Alison from the devastated bush.

'Wind's dropped,' Frank said, looking around also. 'It's just a breeze now.'

Several people stood around the barbecue—the men were taking it in turns to patrol for spot fires in pairs now—and Steve had lit a gas lamp, which hissed faintly as it gave off its white light. In the house, he and Jackie had lit candles, too. The naked flames spooked all of them, but were preferable to darkness. Eddie had deemed it his duty to keep an eye on them. He hobbled around on his sprained ankle, and no one argued because they could all see how much he craved to be useful.

Joan must have been back and forth at least a dozen times. With help from Deirdre and Midori, she'd made her scones and her apple crumble—'But I won't bake that until later'—as well as bringing pots of tea to those who remained in the house. Now she had the spaghetti sauce reheating on the fire, and water almost boiled in a big pot for cooking the pasta.

Checking on Jackie, Jerry and Sarah, Alison found them all gratefully sipping big mugs of Joan's tea. Jackie looked ill at ease. 'This hurts, going down,' she said. 'My chest hurts.'

'I want you resting, Jackie,' Alison said. 'It's not your job to look after everyone. Not even the dogs. And I want you to wait until the tea cools before you drink it. If your throat is burnt, you don't want any more heat on it. Have more water first. Breathe for me.'

I need some equipment. Anything. A stethoscope.

'Cold tea. Yum. OK, breathe?' Jackie obediently did so. After a couple of gulps, she coughed harshly, and Alison heard the way she was wheezing. Still mild. As long as it didn't get any worse…

'No sign of the baby?'

'It's being very good,' Jackie said. 'It knows when to stay put. I'm predicting it's going to be a very easy-care child.'

'Are you feeling much movement, Jackie?'

Even though Alison had tried to ask the question in a casual way, Jackie suddenly went still. 'You think the baby's being *too* good. You think—'

'I'm sure it's fine.' Because what in heaven's name could they do if it wasn't? 'But I'd like you to lie quietly for half an hour and make a note of any movements you can feel.'

'Yes. Yes, of course. I'm sure it's been moving, but— Yes.'

Alison went back out to the barbecue just as Frank and Steve announced that they were going to check on the stock. They'd already watered the two horses and fed them a couple of carrots. The men headed for the house and came past again a few minutes later, wielding bright flashlights and talking to the three dogs who trotted beside them.

Everyone was silent as they watched the two disappear into the blackness of the paddock that fronted the dry river. The flashlight beams bounced around as they walked, showing the occasional flick of a dog's tail or leg in the light. No one said anything about it, but no one could imagine that the cattle would still be alive.

Alison had seen a dead bird fall from the sky that afternoon, just a few yards from where she'd been standing. When? She couldn't remember, hadn't thought of it until this minute when it had popped back into her mind, an isolated piece of memory like a single movie frame. She didn't want to think about the animal life lost in the inferno—could only tell herself that at least it would have happened quickly.

'My husband Ron would have been a hero today, if he'd

been here,' Joan announced suddenly, breaking the silence. Frank and Steve were out of sight now, no more beams of light, no sound from the dogs.

'Would he, Joan?' Nico answered, encouraging her courteously.

'Oh, yes! He was a country boy, a volunteer in the rural fire service. Loved camping. Took me and the boys out all the time, to the Flinders in South Australia, the Cooper at Innamincka, the Birdsville Track, all sorts of places, when the roads were still rough as anything.' She blinked back tears. 'Miss him. Silly. Ten years. Keep thinking of what I'll tell him about the fire today, as if he's sitting at home, waiting to hear it. Anyway. Silly,' she repeated. 'Let's get that spaghetti into the water. Got to feed everyone.'

'Let me do it, Joan.' Again it was Nico, speaking in an oddly gentle voice and coaxing her aside.

'No. You've worked hard already.'

'I'm Italian,' he told her in his musical accent. 'Spaghetti is my area. I would not be a proper man if I let you do it. More to the point, you would overcook it and it would be inedible.' He grinned.

Joan giggled, and Alison felt her own heart lurch. That smile of his. So warm and open and alive. So sexy and seductive, even though that wasn't Nico's intent. She couldn't have responded to it so strongly, she felt, if it had been just another weapon in a deliberately honed male arsenal of techniques to make a woman melt.

He probably had no idea that his smile still arrowed with such perfect accuracy into her heart, the way it always had.

He heaped three packets of spaghetti into the pot, then crouched beside the fire and tangled the long strands of pasta with a barbecue fork until they were soft enough not to stick together. He looked as if he was quite at home and taking everything in stride. The heat that was still draining and oppressive, so that the last place you wanted to be was in front of an open fire. The stench of smoke. The motley collection of strangers forced together. The danger and hard work and physical discomfort. Even the old work jeans of Steve's that he was wearing, now blackened with charcoal and ash, sat on him as if he was used to them.

He'd always been adaptable.

Much more so than I was, Alison found herself thinking.

She had been so narrow back then. So frightened of failure, so bad at operating anywhere outside her comfort zone of hospital-based medicine. She didn't think she could have gone off to Sierra Leone with Médecins Sans Frontières. She didn't think she could have studied medicine in an unfamiliar country and been accepted as a casual member of the student group, the way Nico had been. In his position she'd surely have hidden behind the Conti name, and not made the effort to really connect.

His cheerful ability to adapt had been one of the things she'd loved about him seven years ago, and it began to stir her respect again now, taking her straight into deep water. Had she ever really escaped?

The way she'd kissed him a couple of hours ago suggested she hadn't.

What had that kiss really meant?

'We don't have a colander,' he said. 'Alison, will you hold the lid in place while I tip it and drain it this way? We will do it now, because it will cook a little more in its own heat on the way to the house. We'll use the water to douse this fire.'

'It's done its job, hasn't it?' Rich agreed. 'I'd be edgy about leaving it…which doesn't make sense when I see how many other burning tree stumps there are all around us.'

'Let's do what we can. I could not pour this precious water on open ground. Not tonight.'

Nico and Alison stood close together, her right arm crossed over his as she kept the lid in place with a padded pot-holder while he poured. The steaming water made ash hiss up from the fire and Alison had to hold her breath so she didn't draw it into her already filthy lungs. Some of the steam billowed around to the burn at the back of her leg and made it sting harder. She ought to look at it soon, she realised, but the pain didn't seem important right now.

The pot was big and heavy, and Nico's forearms knotted with effort as he held it, drawing her gaze. Her instinctive female response to his physical strength shocked her with its intensity.

Joan stepped forward to bring the second pot, containing the sauce, but Nico told her, 'No, Joan. Please, call Troy over and he can do it. It is too heavy for you. He's ready for a break from patrol. I will take over while he eats, and he must spend some time with Sarah, too.'

'My turn to patrol as well,' Rich said. 'Sam's busting his guts. And he's using too much hose. Water in the tank must be getting very low.'

'When will you eat, Nico?' Alison had to ask.

He shrugged, and did that very Italian-looking upside-down thing with his mouth. 'When it's my turn.'

'The spaghetti will be inedible by then.' Deliberately, she parroted back the word he'd used a few minutes ago.

He grinned at her. 'By then, I'll be too hungry to care.'

Just as they reached the house, they heard the dogs barking, as well as the voices of Frank and Steve. Something else, too, but what was it?

Cows. The lowing and the movement of cattle, slowly heading in this direction. The herd…or some of it…had survived.

Jackie's baby had survived, too. 'I felt three good strong

movements in half an hour, and lots of flutters,' she reported, looking a little more relaxed.

'No contractions?' Alison relaxed, too.

'A couple of squeezes,' Jackie admitted. 'They weren't painful, and they stopped as soon as I stood up.'

'On the subject of your standing up…' Alison said.

'Yes, I know. I'll lie down again soon. Sarah wants to get up, too, but I've said only if she can keep some dinner down.'

'You're much better at looking after other people than at looking after yourself, Jackie.'

'Too much of a country girl.'

In the kitchen, Joan, Midori and Deirdre served out bowls of spaghetti and sauce, as well as the scones that Joan had baked in an iron camp oven, buried in a nest of coals that had been a fence-post a few hours ago. The scones were still warm, with butter oozing into them and a little dab of sharp Cheddar cheese on top. Midori grabbed one off the top of the pile with a mischievous shrug, then nodded as she tasted it.

Different to what she was used to. Not bad.

It was hard to know what else she was thinking, what she would say if she could communicate. She must have been even more terrified than everyone else during the worst of the fire-storm, surely, but she'd kept it to herself. She'd mimed a question about telephones at one point, after the worst danger was over, and Deirdre had somehow communicated that they were cut off, but that a message would hopefully have got through to Dr Hiromichi earlier, via the fire service, the tour company and the hotel.

Not many people sat down to eat. Alison went out onto the veranda, with a bowl in one hand and a scone in the other, to watch Frank, Steve and the dogs approaching with the herd.

'How many did we lose?' Rich yelled, when they got close enough.

'None that I could see,' Steve yelled back. 'Found a pod of kangaroos there, too. There's that cut-away section of creek bank at the bend, three metres high at one point. They must have all sheltered there and the fire leapt right over them so fast they didn't get burnt. There was so little fuel on the ground. That could be what saved them.'

'You're going to hand-water them?'

'Waterhole's almost dried up. Leave it for the wildlife. We're going to have to buy feed for this lot.'

'They look a bit subdued.'

'So did the kangaroos. Wouldn't you be?'

'There's hot food up,' Rich said. 'Bloody good, too.'

'Going to get the animals settled first.' Steve and Frank began to hand-water the herd, who milled around the men, stretching their necks and lolling out their parched tongues while water poured directly in from buckets and a hose connected to the rainwater tank. The pressure in the hose looked low.

Jackie came out to see what was happening, and insisted on wielding a bucket, too, until Alison abandoned her half-eaten spaghetti and raced across the ruined fence after less than a minute to say forcefully, 'I'll swap with you. I can't look at this. Steve, tell your wife she can't do this.'

'Listen to her, Jackie,' he said. 'She's a doctor, and she's right.'

And Jackie gave up the fight with suspicious ease, while still insisting, 'I'm feeling fine, now. My throat's not hurting much at all. The baby kicked again a minute ago.'

'What if it kicks a cow and the cow kicks back, love?' Steve growled.

Alison soon decided she didn't like cows. 'This assignment is way out of my comfort zone, Daisy, do you realise?' she told one of them.

The animals dropped their heads and pushed at her, impatient for their turn with the bucket, threatening to knock her over or squeeze the air from her lungs between their hot, wall-like sides, and she had that half-hysterical urge to laugh again.

Is this me? Is this real? It can't be!

Nico was laughing.

At her.

The wind had almost completely died away, and streams of embers no longer eddied out of the glowing tree stumps—tiny, insidious enemies that could infiltrate the house and destroy it while one man's back was turned. Danger remained, vigilance was still needed, but it was all less urgent now.

Nico had time to laugh, the sound a deep, delicious vibration in his chest.

'What?' Alison said, glaring at him. His eyes were alive…hot.

'You're doing a great job there. Having fun?'

'Having a ball.' A big cow nose nudged at her half-empty bucket and she got the contents full in the stomach. Since she was already unutterably filthy and still damp and too hot, it hardly seemed to matter. It was just…annoying. 'Do you want a drink, or do you not, Buttercup?' she told the beast. 'Your turn, Nico?'

'No, thanks.' He was still laughing, and she couldn't help laughing, too.

It's not possible I'm actually having fun here…

'I'll just enjoy the show,' Nico finished.

'You're teasing me.'

'Wondering if you like it.'

'I don't.' She paused, and thought, and rashly chose honesty. 'I don't want to like it. But I always used to.'

'Did you?' He was still smiling, watching her with a quizzical look on his face. 'You used to frown at me sometimes.'

'Because I was such a ball of tension I couldn't always let go right away. When I did frown, you ignored me and kept on with the teasing.'

'Because I wanted to unwind the ball of tension a little, and that seemed like the best way.'

She had to laugh, the sound bursting out and filling her body with pleasure. 'It was an excellent way. I liked it, even when I pretended not to. And I still do.'

'Pretend?'

'Like it. Need it,' she added, with way too much honesty for her own good.

He didn't answer. Another cow butted her in the stomach. Poor thing. It was just parched, that was all, it's throat seared by smoke just the way hers was. It could smell the water and it couldn't wait.

She didn't realise that Nico was still watching her until she heard his voice again, pitched just above the persistent lowing of the animals.

'Can we find a chance to talk, do you think?' he said.

'Aren't we talking now?' Not a very clever thing to say, because she knew this wasn't the kind of talking he meant.

His answer was steady and patient. 'I would prefer less of an audience. Something has happened, Alison. Something I never expected, and I want to find out if it's only—I have so many questions about—No, I really can't talk here.'

She let herself look at him. 'No, OK. You haven't eaten yet, have you?'

'Not yet.'

'Do that. By then, I'll be finished here and we can…find somewhere. Just walk, or something.'

'Because it's such a perfect night for a stroll?' he drawled.

'Yes. Particularly with such beautiful moonlight,' she agreed in the same tone, because, of course, nothing in the sky was visible through the haze of smoke.

You could make a nice metaphor out of that, if you wanted to. Nothing in her heart was visible through the haze of what Nico's body did to her. Nothing in her future was visible through the haze of what she felt right now.

But Alison wasn't going to go in for that kind of emotional poetry tonight.

Too dangerous, by far.

CHAPTER SEVEN

NICO and Alison met on the veranda—the same part of it where they'd sheltered during the few minutes when the full force of the fire-storm had raged. Everyone had eaten now, and in the house Alison could faintly hear Joan and Deirdre talking as they cleared up the kitchen. Twice they'd told Jackie to lie down, but she kept reappearing.

Suspicious about it, Alison had asked her a few minutes ago, 'So, what's happening, Jackie?'

'Oh, contractions whenever I lie down. They're not painful at all. And they go away as soon as I get up.'

'Which is why you keep getting up?'

'Uh, yes. They can't be labour, then, can they?'

Let me just page Dr Obstetrics Expert down on our maternity floor and he can come up and check you out…

'No,' Alison answered firmly. 'It's not labour.'

The veranda seemed oddly peaceful and private, in a different universe from the one where Alison and Nico had clung and yelled and kissed a few hours ago, even though it was the same place.

'Shall we try a walk, then?' Nico said. 'Just get away from the house for a little while? I've brought a flashlight.'

'I do feel restless,' Alison agreed. 'Surely I must be tired…'

'But somehow you don't feel it. I know.'

They stepped off the veranda and onto the burned ground, with its thick crust of bitter ash, then began to walk along the farm track in the direction of the road. Nico clicked on the flashlight, making a circle of light just beyond their feet.

106

It lit up the way ahead but left the two of them in darkness. Although he made no attempt to touch her, Alison sensed how near he was with almost every nerve-ending.

This shouldn't feel so intimate, but it did and she knew he was aware of it, too. Her stomach felt fluttery with both expectancy and fear. It wasn't hard to imagine this ending in a crashing argument and a realisation that the chemical attraction between them could go nowhere. It was much harder to tell herself that an argument would probably be the best outcome.

'We used to feel this way during our internship,' Alison said. 'Sometimes I still do, if we have an especially frantic day.' She wasn't willing to cut to the important stuff just yet. Maybe there'd turn out to be no important stuff anyhow.

'I don't suppose you go wandering around the streets of Chicago at midnight to walk it off?'

'My gym stays open till eleven. I often go for a late-night swim. At that hour, I'm sometimes the only person in the pool.'

'It sounds a little lonely. Have you become too successful to need a private life, Alison?'

'Not at all.' On the defensive already! Had he wanted that? 'I have friends, colleagues I get on well with. My mother and I are very close. I wanted her to come out here with me, but she wouldn't take the time off. Her cleaning company is growing by leaps and bounds.'

'Corporate clients?'

'No, mostly smaller businesses. She recruits her staff locally and that way cuts down on their travel time, which means she can—Is this what you want to talk about?'

'I want to find out what's important to you now. It sounds as if your mother is.'

'She always has been. She sacrificed so much for me, *wanted* so much for me.'

'Yes, that was always obvious. I think she transferred a lot of that to you. I used to want to get you out from under it sometimes. That's why I teased you so much, and why I brought you coffee and—'

'Told me to relax when assignment deadlines got extended, made me eat fruit, took me on all these crazy outings, pretended you needed help with pronouncing English medical terms...'

She was laughing as she spoke, remembering all the ways he'd spoilt her, remembering how surprised she'd been at first, and then how happy it had made her, how she'd always felt able to be her best self when they were together. Oh, oh, she'd loved him so much for all of that! The feeling came flooding back, astonishingly fresh and strong and vital after so long, and she had to struggle to keep up her light tone as she finished, 'So I'd come to your apartment to drill you through them...'

'Bronchiectasis, chylothorax, kyphoscoliosis,' he intoned, in an exaggerated parody of his light accent.

'But when I did that all you really wanted, it turned out, was to fill me with Italian food.'

'There were one or two other things I wanted when you came to my apartment,' he reminded her. 'But, yes, you never looked after yourself properly. It used to drive me crazy. I wanted to call up your mother and tell her, "Feed your daughter! Buy fabric softener and stain soaker for her laundry, and tissues and bath crystals and moisturiser, because she forgets half those things every week!"'

'I still forget them, but not as often.'

'"Tell her how brave and strong and clever she is, because most of the time she doesn't seem to know. Above all, introduce her to the concept of watching a rented video in fluffy slippers!"'

'Which she couldn't, because she never did that herself

back then. She's gotten a little better at spoiling herself now, but I'm the one teaching her!'

'And is she happy with what you have?'

She'd have liked me to make a brilliant marriage. With you.

'She's very proud of me, even though she doesn't say it in words.'

'She should be proud, and she should say it in words. Why this tough love? Why hold back?'

'Well, no, she was right in what she always used to say. I had a good brain and it would be wrong not to make the best use of it. What about your parents, Nico?' she added quickly. 'They're well and happy, I hope.'

'There's a lot to catch up on, isn't there?' he murmured, half to himself. 'You would have no way of knowing this. It turned out my father was ill that summer.' She didn't need to ask him which summer he meant. Their Italian summer, of course. Their only summer.

'Not seriously, I hope,' she said.

'Yes, it was quite serious. Lung cancer.'

'Oh, Nico! I'm sorry to hear it.'

'I don't know if you remember how bad-tempered and difficult he was. Well, of course not, you'd have had nothing to compare it with, since you hadn't known him before.'

'I did find him a little…intimidating,' she admitted. She'd been thoroughly convinced that Nico's father didn't like her.

'He knew something was wrong, but I think it's very hard for some men—and particularly men of that generation—to acknowledge any kind of weakness, and they perceive illness to be just as much a weakness as any other kind of failing.'

'That's true.' She thought briefly of Jerry, resting inside.

'For months he tried to hide from us and from himself that he wasn't feeling well, but finally my mother guessed and made him take the right steps. The surgery was successful, but he wasn't able to stop smoking completely and he's had a recurrence this past year. Somehow, this time I'm more concerned.'

'Because he's that much older?'

'Because he's behaving out of character this time around! Not the same belligerence. He's become—this is going to sound strange—tolerant and sentimental and softer towards us all, and that's what concerns me more than the bad temper and the denial ever did. He actually told me a few weeks ago that I should follow my heart!'

The whole universe seemed to jolt. 'So you are in love?' she asked lightly.

'No, oh, no, I didn't mean that. We were talking about my professional future. I want to go back to practising medicine, and…' He sighed. 'I don't know if this makes any sense, Alison, but it…uh…terrifies me, if I'm honest, that he's not standing in my way.'

'Yes,' she answered, feeling his emotion. 'I see. Of course. And how is your mother handling it?'

'She's softened, too. I've never seen her so tender with him before, or him so tender with her. They've always behaved true to the Italian stereotype. Very happy to yell at each other, but there's none of that any more.'

He didn't go on, and she understood the implications of what he'd said. She didn't want to come out with trite words of optimism or sympathy, so she took his hand instead. It felt warm and dry and a little rough. Were those blisters she could feel at the tops of his palms, from that grinding work with the pick, hours ago?

Their silence lasted for several minutes. They reached the road, and Nico swept the flashlight beam along it in both directions, revealing the drastically changed landscape, ghostly and grey and silent, apart from the occasional crash of a falling tree, sometimes close and at others much further away.

'In a way I prefer the darkness,' Alison said. 'The places where the coals are still glowing at least seem alive. Under the flashlight beam, everything goes so dead. The aftermath and the ash don't seem like part of my home planet at all. We're on one of Jupiter's moons, or something.'

'Yes, it's bizarre. It's not an experience I ever expected to have.'

'We should probably go back.'

'Yes, we should.'

They turned and retraced their steps. More silence. Their hands were still linked. Eventually, Nico said, 'Tell me the real reason why you haven't got married. Not that it-just-never-happened thing that everyone says.'

You're the reason. Everything you made me feel when we were lovers. Everything you made me feel when you turned away.

Could she say that?

Could she strip herself bare to such an extent?

No.

'Don't you think people mean it when they say that?' she asked him lightly. 'Don't you think that sometimes life just never puts the right person in front of you?'

'You're not a passive person, Alison, and you've always had so much more courage than you know. If you wanted something and life didn't put it there, you'd go out, you'd keep looking until you found it, you'd grab hold of it and bring it home.'

'Clubbed unconscious by my cave-woman weapon, you mean?'

'No, I don't mean that at all. It wasn't necessarily a criticism.'

'Not necessarily. You're hedging your bets.' She dropped

his hand and looked at his steady profile. 'In some circumstances, you'd consider it a criticism.'

'In some circumstances, I would,' he agreed, with an edge.

They reached the veranda again, but reached an unspoken consensus not to go in just yet. Nico switched off the flashlight, and the softness of candlelight spilled onto the veranda through the windows instead.

'The cow pats in the paddock were flaming after the firefront went through, did you notice that?' Alison said.

'I noticed the noise more than anything. I couldn't believe the deafening roar. I couldn't hear a word of what you said while we stood here.'

'I know. And I couldn't hear you.'

'Then is there time for us to say it over again now? Do we want to?' He sounded cool and a little mocking, which drew her gaze to his face.

Her eyes had adjusted to the soft near-darkness now, and she could see the ambivalence in his expression. Could he be feeling the same painful mix of emotions that she was? She couldn't even have named them all. Hope, fear, cynicism, wariness...

'Say them over?' She made a helpless sound. 'I don't think we could. I don't think we'd mean any of it in the same way.'

'You have an inkling, then...'

She faced him with a steadier focus. 'You said you loved me, and you never stopped. I heard that part. But that's what people say when they think they're about to die. They cling to things that...' She sighed. 'Might even be true, in one sense, but that doesn't actually solve anything. We can't undo the past. And love isn't...isn't like a fire-storm. It doesn't just sweep through and—You sent me packing seven years ago.'

'That's how you see it?'

'Yes. You just arranged for me to get delivered to the airplane in a strange country, with no explanation, because I hadn't managed to impress your parents the way you'd hoped. Or that's what I had to assume, since you never said. It's something I never understood, Nico. Something I still don't understand, even now. That's not what people do when they love someone.'

'That's not what happened.'

'It is what happened. It shocked me so much because it didn't seem like you. And you never called. You just…' she made a snatching gesture '…removed yourself from my life.'

'That's not what happened,' he repeated, his voice suddenly low and intense.

Her own voice rose in response, too high and too loud. 'Then what did happen? Because at the point where I flew to Italy, if someone had asked for my prediction on what would have happened to us seven years later, I'd have said we'd be married. Probably with a toddler and a new baby on the way. Close. Still knowing exactly how to make each other laugh, how to bring out the best in each other, the way we always did. The way we did before Italy.'

Lord, even now she could almost see it, little snatches of a shared life, viewed in her mind like movie stills. Nico and Alison on their wedding day, their honeymoon, celebrating her first pregnancy, and the birth of their child.

'I would never have thought,' she went on, 'that we'd be meeting up like this—near strangers with hostile memories. So something happened. And if it wasn't that my behaviour failed your parents' test, then tell me what it was.'

'It wasn't what you did, it was what you didn't feel.'

'*Didn't* feel?'

'You want me to put it bluntly?'

'Please!'

'You wanted my money, my title, my position, my connections, not me, and I didn't see it until you came to Italy.'

'*What?*'

'You were so stiff and unnatural, Alison. My father told me to look at the whole thing clearly, and that's what I saw. Admittedly—and *he* admitted it—my parents saw potential problems in the conflict between our different ambitions and duties as well, but that wouldn't have made a difference if I'd been sure you really cared. But when I looked, I couldn't see it. You just couldn't sustain the performance under more challenging conditions.'

'That's not true!'

'You were ambitious, and your mother pushed you. You'd worked so hard, with such focus, to get as far as you had in medicine. It's understandable that an ambitious marriage would also be in your game plan, and that you would pursue it in the same way. Tightening your fists and rolling yourself into a tight little ball of determined wanting, that sometimes seemed inept and vulnerable and endearing and at others seemed…' he sighed. '…hopelessly shallow. You were inexperienced. You were influenced so much by what your mother wanted.'

Alison swallowed a profane word. 'Are you actually making excuses for me?'

'You were young. We both were.'

'You are making excuses!'

He ignored her. 'And when I tried to question you about it, you obviously felt put under a microscope and got even worse. I'd known quite a lot of women whose goal was a wealthy marriage—gold-diggers is the English term, isn't it?—and I've known quite a few more since. Sometimes it doesn't matter, when a man's own interest is equally superficial.'

He gave a very worldly, European shrug, and Alison gave a squeak of outrage. She couldn't find the cutting words she wanted at all.

'You think to yourself, OK, so they're using me,' he continued. 'I'll use them, we'll smile about it and that's that. No one gets hurt because no one is vulnerable, no one is in any doubt as to what's happening. You were different, because it took me too long to guess. I thought you were not that type at all, and by the time I did guess that you and women like that were sisters under the skin...' He stopped. 'It hurt. I was vulnerable. Because I loved you.'

'I loved *you*! Nico, I *loved* you!'

'Did you? Are you so sure of that?' He studied her face. For proof, apparently.

'Yes!' she almost shouted. 'I was intimidated by your money and your position, not attracted to those things! I was never a gold-digger. But I could see as soon as I came to Italy that I wasn't the wife your parents wanted for you, and that only made my behaviour worse. Were we so out of touch with each other that we could both get it so wrong?'

'The evidence of seven years speaks for itself, I think.'

'Oh, it was doomed, wasn't it?' She pressed her hands to her hot cheeks. 'Oh, it's funny, in hindsight.'

'Is it?'

'Yes. Both of us suffering for no apparent reason. Both of us too much under the influence of what our parents wanted. Italian sons and American daughters of single moms tend to be dutiful!'

'And that's a bad thing?'

'No. Not always. But in this case...' She shook her head. 'Both of us swept off our feet by inept first love that can't last because the slightest thing is going to crack everything apart and shatter any possibility of communication. I'd mourn such an awful misunderstanding, except I think that if we hadn't misunderstood each other over that, we would have done so over something else.'

'With equally disastrous results?'

'Exactly. We must have been very young.'

'And now we're very cynical,' he suggested.

'No. Just wiser. Rueful, rather than cynical.'

She tried to smile up at him and that was a mistake. She couldn't look away, and he didn't want her to.

'But the attraction is still there, Alison,' he said softly. 'Don't you think that's strange? Should we be rueful about that?'

'Ruefulness seems the appropriate response. And what are our other choices?' she drawled.

'To explore,' he suggested. 'To seize the time we have and make the very best of it.'

'How?' she challenged him sharply. 'How on earth are you suggesting we do that?'

She knew as soon as she'd finished speaking that he wasn't going to answer her in words.

CHAPTER EIGHT

THEIR kiss was less urgent than it had been while the fire-front had raged through.

But it was more important.

Was that possible?

Nico pinned his hands on her shoulders, and Alison instinctively closed her eyes, feeling the balls of his thumbs caressing the stress-tightened muscles above her shoulder blades even before she felt the touch of his mouth.

He always used to do this for her, she remembered. He'd immediately pick up when she was tense, and he'd massage her until she turned into laughing, quivering chocolate mousse and the stress-releasing massage became a shared quest for sensual fulfillment which left her even more relaxed than before. So wordlessly happy, too.

When the touch of his mouth did come, she forgot about everything else.

He kissed like heaven.

His mouth was soft yet firm, and he was very sure that she wanted this. He wasn't wrong. She surrendered her whole soul to it at once, parted her lips, tasted him, wrapped her arms around him and didn't care about anything else in the world. Not the taint of smoke in the air and on his skin, not the fatigue that could take hold if she let it, not the concerns about Jerry and Sarah and Jackie and the others that buzzed in the back of her mind like radio static.

This was where she wanted to be. This was what she wanted to feel.

Nico.

His body was hard against hers, leaving her in no doubt as to his strength. She'd seen it today, too, when he'd helped to bury the plastic pipe beneath a protective layer of earth. She didn't know why his strength should feel so important. Some elemental awareness of his maleness and her contrasting female softness, she thought.

It was so good and so right to be aware of it somehow. To be able to glory in all the ways they were different, to celebrate the astonishing miracle of making a connection across so many barriers of time and culture and gender and background.

His strong, square jaw felt rough with his faint new growth of beard. She touched it, the sensitive skin of her fingertips alive to the complex, delicious texture and to the contrast it made with his soft, perfect mouth.

'No one else has ever made me feel like this,' she whispered, barely taking her mouth from his. 'I don't know why. But no one ever has. If you want to know why I'm not married, why the relationships I've had since I knew you haven't worked out, that's why. Because I loved you, and you hurt me, and I couldn't forget either of those things. No one else has ever, ever made me feel anything like this,' she repeated.

This unique combination of utter rightness and heart-thumping adventure. The sense of *wanting* the challenge of a man who was so different, and yet exulting in the discoveries they made about all the ways they were the same. The feeling of coming home to a whole new world.

It was a potent connection that she'd never been able to explain to herself seven years ago, and couldn't explain now.

'No. I know,' he answered. 'I know. This is why it would

be so wrong to let it go. Whatever we are risking tonight, Alison, I want to take that risk. I don't want to hold back. I don't care about tomorrow. There was a time today when we didn't even think tomorrow would come.'

'Yes.' She shivered, remembering how right it had felt to be sharing that terrifying time with him and nobody else.

'If we were both wrong seven years ago,' he whispered, 'then let's try to make it right now, let's find out if the right passion is still there.'

He kissed her again, his mouth hungrier and more demanding now. Alison pressed herself against him, wanting his hardness and his body heat, giddy with happiness. She could hardly breathe. She pillowed her head on his shoulder, smelling the smoke on his skin that couldn't drown the scent that was uniquely his.

He touched her as if he couldn't get enough, and she let herself melt against his hands, feeling every point of contact as a stinging throb of sensation that echoed all through her body. 'Make love to me,' she whispered, and it seemed like another voice speaking, not hers.

'I want to,' he answered, his breath hot in her ear. 'Oh, I want to.'

He branded her jawline with his mouth and she twisted and arched to give him more. She ran her fingers up through his hair, loving the way it grew from his perfectly shaped head. 'Yes. Please.'

'But where can we go?' he said.

'I—I don't know, Nico. I don't care. We'll find somewhere.' He laughed, and she pulled back a little and looked at him, stroking his face once more. 'How bad did that sound?'

'It sounded good. So good.'

'It sounded a little, um, more desperate than I meant it to.'

'Let me kiss you again, and you'll see how desperate I am, too. Desperate…and patient, because kissing you feels so good I'm in no hurry for it to stop.'

This time he didn't content himself with just her face. He kissed her neck and her ear and her collar-bone, ran his hands possessively over the curves of her breasts and hips, and slid them between her thighs.

Ten minutes later, she told him, 'You've proved your point.'

'Remind me what my point was again?' He bumped his nose against hers, and printed the teasing ghost of a kiss on her lips. His mossy, chocolaty eyes held a caress in their depths.

'That you were in no hurry for this part to stop.'

'Oh, that's right, no hurry…' A second later he stiffened, suddenly alert to something new. 'What's that noise?'

'Someone in the house?' Alison hadn't even heard a noise. Her senses had gone giddy and strange, the way they had that afternoon. The pulsing core deep in her body overrode everything else.

'No, it's coming from…' He stopped and listened. His whole body had changed, gone on the alert. 'It's an engine! A vehicle.'

'It can't be.' She didn't want it to be. Against all logic, she didn't want the outside world again yet. She wanted to stay in this blackened, smoke-tainted paradise for hours longer. Just a few sweet hours, please. With Nico.

'It definitely is.' He narrowed his eyes and listened harder. 'A vehicle engine. Not a car, something more powerful. It's getting closer and louder. I think. It has to be.'

'Does that mean the emergency services have reopened the road?'

'Frank's been listening to the radio. The fire's still out of control and running parallel to it. I can't imagine they'd allow regular traffic through yet. And who would want to drive it this late at night? Any sane person would wait until morning now.'

With their arms around each other, they watched and waited, listening to the engine noise getting slowly louder. It sounded grinding and laboured and not quite right. Alison thought she heard a shout at one point also.

Richard Porter had heard the new sounds now. He appeared on the veranda, his eyes trained on the black, invisible road through the darkness. Nico dropped his arms at last, and Alison felt bereft. Hopeful, too. It was a strange mix.

'Sounds like a truck,' Richard said. 'Someone from the next property maybe? They're not here that much. City people. Taking their time, whoever it is. Vehicle's moving at a crawl from what I can hear. I'm going to get a light, go out to the end of our track, see what's going on.'

When he reappeared, Frank was with him.

'Got to be almost at our mailbox now,' he said. 'They might not know we're here. Emergency vehicle maybe, checking local properties? I radioed earlier to say we were OK, but could do with getting a few people evacuated. I was told we'd have to wait. They sounded pretty stretched. Didn't think we'd get any attention before morning.'

Already disappearing into the darkness, with his son swinging the flashlight beam ahead of them, Frank called the last sentence back over his shoulder.

Nico looked beyond the men and said, 'I can see headlights out on the road…swinging around… I think they're coming this way.'

'Oi!' Frank began to call, breaking into a run and waving his arms.

The big vehicle ground its way laboriously along the ash-covered farm track. It seemed to detour at a couple of points, where Alison knew that burnt-out trees had fallen across the track. She and Nico had skirted them on foot earlier.

When the vehicle emerged from the smoke-laden darkness, she and Nico could both see that it was a Rural Fire Service truck—a tanker unit, she'd heard Steve or someone call it today—and that Frank and Rich were hitching a ride on the outside.

They could have walked faster, Alison felt.

Rich must have agreed. He leapt off again and came towards them at a loping run. He sounded breathless. 'Got some injured firies on board,' he said. 'And a bit of equipment. Ambulance got burned out further up the road. These guys grabbed whatever they could get their hands on out of the back of it, but they didn't have much time.'

'What kind of injuries?' Nico asked at once, while a shiver ran down Alison's spine.

'Smoke inhalation, a slashed leg, and a couple of them are pretty badly burned.'

'Are the ambulance paramedics with them?' Alison asked. 'Because that might be useful…'

'Uh, no.' He frowned. 'I think it was a sticky situation. No one was thinking too clearly. Paramedics went in another vehicle, although one of these guys—one of the ones in best shape—told me he did five years as a critical care nurse in Sydney before he moved down here.'

Alison saw Nico nod, as her own ears pricked up. If the man was indeed in good shape, they could use his help.

'This lot got overtaken by the front later on, on a side road,' Rich was saying, 'while they were checking a containment line.'

'I am guessing it was breached,' Nico said.

'Uh, yeah, just a bit,' Rich said. His tone said that this was the understatement of the year. 'Truck got damaged and they couldn't get it started at first. Top speed is currently ten kilometres an hour.'

'Which is why it's taken them a while to get here.' Alison nodded.

'And why they're not going any further tonight.'

'They shouldn't anyhow,' Nico said. 'Not if the road is still under threat. We can treat their injuries here.'

If the firefighters had managed to grab the right equipment from the ambulance, Alison amended, but she didn't say it aloud. Nico, more used to working in primitive conditions, sounded more optimistic than she dared to feel.

There were seven men and one woman in the Fire Service truck. They climbed out slowly, looking filthy and exhausted and dazed—too much so for speech. One man apparently needed the support of two others in order to walk. All of them were showing degrees of respiratory distress, some more than others. It was evident in their pale skin, soot-stained nostrils, rapid breathing, hoarse voices and harsh coughing.

'I'm Mark Pitman, and I've got good nursing experience,' one of them said at once to Nico and Alison, his breathing effortful but deep. 'Did you get told?'

'Yes, we did,' Alison answered.

'Thanks, Mark,' Nico said. 'Good to know. Get some rest now, until we need you.'

Alison stepped closer to Nico. 'Let's talk about how we're going to handle this.'

'Yes. Is it fair to move Jackie and Steve out of their bedroom?' he asked in a rapid undertone. He touched her arm, reclaiming their intimacy, reminding her of it, even though they both knew it was gone now, and they might not get it back.

'I think we have to.' Her instincts as a doctor had kicked in. There was a relief in that, an adrenalin rush, a reminder that she was strong. She found the fact easier to believe now, for some reason. The passage of the fire? Or Nico, and the talk they'd had, the realisation that they'd both made mistakes? 'It's nearest the bathroom, where we've set up what we already have, such as it is,' she said.

'Such as it is,' he echoed.

'Can we get their most able-bodied to direct Steve and Rich to the equipment and bring it in?' she suggested.

'Not Mark. He should get cleaned up, get food and water, ready to step in when we're more organised.'

'I'm praying for IV gear and fluids, pain relief, antibiotics…'

'A stethoscope might be nice,' Nico said.

'Oh, wouldn't it! Let's think. Swallowing may be a problem for some of them, which makes oral fluid delivery harder…'

'You don't subscribe to the thinking that fluids are going to increase the oedema in the larynx—'

'Resulting in airway occlusion,' she finished for him. 'It's a possibility, yes, but I think the fluid loss is the bigger concern, especially when we're dealing with burns. If we get plummeting blood pressure and shock—'

'Deferring to your expertise,' Nico said.

'I'll be deferring to yours, if they haven't rescued the right gear.' She gripped his hand. 'Can we really work like this? It's so totally not what I'm used to.'

'We can,' he told her almost curtly, 'when we have no choice. Believe me.'

He was already moving towards the group of shattered volunteers. How long had they been on the job? Alison wondered. How long since they'd eaten? Had their drinking water held out?

Burns wasn't her area. Smoke inhalation, yes, but not burns. She tried to remember the Parkland formula for fluid treatment for burns victims. Weight by body area burnt by... She'd have to think about it in a minute.

She grabbed Frank, who let his face show his thoughts for a few fleeting seconds. How much more would they get hit with today? They'd got through the fire, and Jackie hadn't delivered a baby in the middle of it. He didn't want to lose anyone on his watch at this late hour, let alone one of these heroes in their blackened yellow uniforms.

'We're going to set all of them up in Jackie and Steve's room, for efficiency's sake,' she said to him. 'If you think Jackie and Steve won't mind.'

'They'll be fine,' Frank answered. 'It's not like they're going to let themselves take enough of a break to use it, and they can bed down in the baby's room if they want to. I'm going to get on the radio again, see if I can find out what's happening with the fire and the road.'

'Yes, if there's a chance we could get an ambulance...more than one...there are people here who need hospital treatment.'

Nico came back in her direction, carrying something in a special case. 'Is that—?' she began.

'A defibrillator. Makes sense. Most expensive piece of equipment.'

But they both knew it wasn't what they needed now. In

a rural environment like this, it surely wouldn't be an advanced model, in any case.

'I'm told there's IV gear, though,' Nico went on. 'Fluids, oxygen, another nebuliser. Some drugs, but they don't know what. We'll have to look.'

Another period of controlled chaos began. Joan and Deirdre kept up supplies of hot water and the two women were able to sponge clean several minor gashes and grazed limbs under Mark's supervision while Nico and Alison worked over the most serious cases—the ones whose breathing was threatened, or who had sizeable burns. Mark also did a rough triage assessment on his colleagues and gave a reassuring report.

Wall-to-wall beds were set up on the floor in Jackie and Steve's room, using the gear that the volunteers themselves carried with them—thin foam mats and sleeping bags. The burly, filthy firefighters looked incongruous next to the pristine white bassinet already set up in the room just across the corridor, ready for the new baby. Alison threw some bedding for Jackie and Steve into the baby's room, then as a hygiene precaution she grabbed one of the large plastic garbage bags she'd found earlier and covered the bassinet over, before closing the door on the little space.

Going through the salvaged equipment from the ambulance, she found salbutamol but no antibiotics, burns dressings but no painkillers. There, Nico's sparse collection of samples would have to do. And there was a stethoscope. She almost kissed it, then hung it around her neck like a string of garlic for warding off vampires. Precious, precious instrument. She'd never take it for granted again! If Nico wanted to use it, she'd charge him rent!

In Jackie and Steve's bedroom, she set up both nebulisers, for the two firefighters whose breathing seemed most distressed. The one from the ambulance was a nice new model. To a third firie, who went by the nickname of Lefty, she said, 'You're next.'

But he shook his head. 'I'm fine.' His voice was hoarse. 'Been doin' this for twenty years. Fire captain at my shed for ten of 'em. I'll bounce back. Just need to keep on with the water.' He had an opaque plastic bottle in his hand and was taking cautious sips, wincing at the pain that came when he swallowed.

Alison listened to his chest with her precious new instrument. He would definitely need the nebuliser. Had she been wrong to identify this man's treatment as less urgent just because he appeared in less pain and hadn't complained?

She had found an asthma inhaler in the bathroom cabinet—Nico had said he had a couple of newer models in his bag, too, she remembered—and knew that at a pinch the salbutamol could be delivered that way, but suspected it would be an ineffective method with this patient. She showed it to him anyway. 'Ever used one of these before?'

He shook his head.

'Want to give it a try?'

'Told you, I'm fine. Give it to Kim there.'

Alison turned to the lone woman amongst the firefighting crew. She was a strongly built, dark-haired and attractive young woman somewhere in her late twenties, who could still summon a smile. 'Kim?'

'What am I getting?'

'This will ease your breathing if you can get the hang of how to inhale it.'

'Sure, if you show me.' Her voice croaked even more hoarsely than her captain's, and when she held out her right hand Alison saw the way three of her fingers had adhered together. Kim saw it, too. 'Oh. That's right,' she muttered, and switched hands. The left wasn't much better.

Hands…adhesions…scar tissue…loss of mobility and function.

Along with the face and genitals, burnt hands were something you took seriously, no matter how much or how little burned skin there was elsewhere.

Alison heard Nico ask, 'Jackie, do you have plastic cling-film in your kitchen?'

Like Alison, he'd seen that Kim's burns warranted the most urgent attention. She'd burned a sizeable stretch of her back and shoulder as well, and Nico had already cut large swathes of cloth away from the area to facilitate treatment. Meanwhile, two men had charred uniforms clinging to their lower legs which would also need cutting away.

Mark saw her looking in that direction and told her, 'Leave it to me.'

'Look after yourself, too, Mark.'

'I'm fine.'

They were all saying it, even the ones she didn't believe once she'd listened to the way their chests crackled and wheezed. With rapid breathing, fluid loss through the lungs would be greater. They could go into shock. She wasn't going to lessen her vigilance for a while.

She helped Kim to inhale the salbutamol. 'Feeling a bit better,' Kim said almost at once, even though her laboured breathing hadn't given her optimal delivery. As soon as one of the nebulisers was free, she should have another turn with that.

Jerry had been coughing, too, his sleep restless in the armchair he'd stayed in for hours, barring a few short, fretful walks around the house. He would need a check and an update on his medication soon, but for now he'd have to wait.

He came back with the clingfilm. 'Can you set up an IV line for Kim while I'm treating her hands?' he asked Alison quietly. With his body so near, she had to fight the temptation to touch him, just a quick moment of contact, to remind both of them about…well, a lot of things. 'I'm estimating the burn area at eighteen per cent,' he finished, 'which starts to get significant in terms of fluid loss.'

'Especially in concert with greater than usual loss from the lungs,' she agreed. 'If you're wrapping her hands, you want the IV to be—?'

'Ante-cubital, yes.'

In the crook of the elbow, with a wide-bore cannula.

'Right.' Alison summoned the Parkland formula from her tired brain. Two to four mils per kilo per burnt area, with fifty per cent over the first eight hours. Kim would weigh around seventy kilos. Hell. Where was her mental arithmetic? Four times seventy times eighteen divide by two…

Nico got there a few seconds ahead of her. 'Two litres at two-fifty mils per hour.'

As Alison set up the IV, he worked on Kim's hands, carefully separating the adhered fingers with pads of dry, sterile gauze, squeezing a thick, milky antiseptic gel over the burn then wrapping the entire hand in glistening plastic clingfilm.

Kim's peripheral veins were flat and Nico had been right to suggest the crook of the elbow. Her heart rate was elevated, as was her rate of breathing, and Alison suspected her blood pressure must be dropping. She'd closed her eyes. Would she open them again, if she heard her name?

'Kim?' Alison said.

Kim blinked and looked but said nothing.

'Can you tell me what day it is today?'

'Um…' Once more, her eyes closed. She was definitely going into shock, enough to have caused her consciousness to drop a point or two on the scale Alison had fixed in her mind after years of use. Thank heavens for the IV and that fluid now going in so nicely, drip, drip, drip.

'You OK…Kimmy?' the fire captain asked.

Hearing the breath he had to draw to get through the short sentence, Alison looked sharply towards him. He was breathing faster now, the corner of his mouth was leaking saliva and his nostrils had begun to flare. Even through the disguising effect of his bulky yellow uniform, she saw the extra effort he needed to put in to get enough air. The muscles across his ribs sucked in, and his throat showed a tracheal tug below the Adam's apple.

'Lefty, I'm going to take your pulse,' she told him, and sure enough it was fast, like his breathing, and she didn't need her trusty stethoscope to detect the croup-like crowing sound that came with every effortful in-breath he took. His trachea hadn't stopped swelling yet, and she knew that it could close off completely with dangerous suddenness. She asked Nico, 'Did we get any airway equipment from the ambulance?'

He looked at Lefty quickly, then answered, 'No. Think we're going to need it?'

'Hope not.'

'If you're…talking about me…I'm…fine,' Lefty said.

But he'd begun to sweat, and Alison could see the panic rising in his face. Without another word, Nico disappeared from the room, and Mark had gone on the alert, too.

'Mate,' he said. 'Don't play the hero, OK?'

Lefty vomited seconds after Nico had gone. Alison just had time to grab a bowl to contain the mess, but the violence of it and the constriction in his throat made the event particularly painful and frightening for him, and when he tried to talk, he couldn't.

OK, his airway was closing fast, and she knew she had to act. Nico knew it, too.

'Scissors,' he said behind her. 'Cleaner than the ones we've been using. Sterilise them?'

'No, there's no time,' she answered urgently.

Lefty was still managing to draw a tiny amount of air, but he was losing the battle. The deadly swelling had almost blocked his larynx. The oesophagus below the larynx wouldn't swell as much, so if they could just get an airway in below that point...

'I need them now! And a pen casing. Now, now, now!' she repeated as she watched her patient subside to the floor. 'He's out for the count.'

Lord, she didn't want to do this, not in these primitive conditions! Where was her scalpel with a guarded blade? Where was her anaesthesia, her sterile tubing, her nursing staff, her artery forceps, her latex gloves?

Her hands felt clumsy and numb as she wrenched open the snap-fasteners on Lefty's uniform and stretched his head back. His chest wasn't moving at all. Aware that every second made a difference, she wasted several of them by being unable to begin. If Nico had pushed her aside and taken control, she wouldn't have protested. She'd have felt deeply relieved.

But he didn't push her aside.

Instead, she heard his voice, measured, calm, efficient.

'Locate your landmarks, Alison.'

'Yes.' She looked up and found him close to her, eyes fixed on her face. The sight calmed and focused her as nothing else could have done, reminded her that she *could* do this, she *was* in control. He'd always been able to do this for her, and right now it felt like nothing less than a miracle. Taking a breath, she looked back at her patient's throat.

'The cricothyroid membrane,' Nico said. 'That's right. There's your thyroid and your cricoid cartilage. You want to be right in between, at the midline. Now, your incision…'

Her voice was crisp again now. 'One point five centimetres.' She opened the scissors, wishing they were sharper and cleaner, and used one blade. Under the circumstances, the incision was gratifyingly tidy.

'Got no artery forceps,' Nico coached again. 'So…'

'Twist the blade to keep the incision open. I'm fine now. Thanks for—'

'Don't mention it. Here's your pen casing. Not as wide as I'd have liked.'

'Thanks.'

She slid it in and down, carefully extracted the scissor blade then waited for chest movement and the sound of air. They didn't come. Lord, there was nothing! 'I wasted too much time,' she said through clenched teeth.

'You didn't. This happens. His chest's not inflating, so get him started,' Nico said. 'Blow into the casing.'

'Right.'

She bent close and put her lips over the thin tube of rigid plastic, blew and waited and blew again, then sat back and heard the whistle of outgoing air. Lefty was breathing. On his own. His chest was moving. Thank heaven. It was a simple matter to attach and tape tubing from the portable oxygen supply to the end of the pen casing.

'Too fast and shallow,' Nico said. 'He's not getting enough oxygen to bring full consciousness back, but he'll be stable at least, and happier if he isn't aware of that bit of plastic sticking out of his throat.'

'I'm sure he will! Let's tape it in place, get him into a better position. He'll need monitoring.'

'You've got me for that,' Mark came in. 'He's my captain and he's a good bloke.' He reached out and took a pulse as soon as he'd spoke, staying quiet while he counted, then reporting, 'For the moment, he's all right.'

'We need to get these people to a hospital as soon as it's safe to get out,' Nico said.

'That has to be soon!'

'I've given a dose of broad-spectrum antibiotic to Kim and this man needs one, too, but that's it, I've got nothing else. They were sample doses from my bag, that's all.'

'I think we've done pretty well,' Alison said. She clutched the stethoscope around her neck like a lifeline, and smiled at Nico.

'We have,' he agreed. 'Let's take a deep breath in case there's more. I am going to take a tour, while you and Mark finish up here. I will see you, OK?'

'It won't be too soon,' she told him, and neither of them cared what Mark thought as they gripped each other's hands and locked their eyes on each other's faces.

CHAPTER NINE

WHEN she left the room some minutes later, still clutching her stethoscope, Alison encountered Nico in the corridor and felt an immediate wash of relief and new strength.

'I was coming to find you,' he said.

'I wasn't lost.'

He laughed. 'Nobody's lost. We've got through the worst, I think. Some people are sleeping. How are Lefty and Kim?'

She ran through a quick list of their vital signs, then added, 'Mark's still keeping a close watch. He told me I should take a break.'

'He's right.' He tried to lift the stethoscope's black tubing from around her neck, but she fought him.

'I'm not letting go of that!'

'Security blanket, Dr Lane?'

'Oh, yeah! And I know this is going to seem about as meaningful as asking whether the Nasdaq index rose or fell today, but...what's the time, Nico, do you have any idea?'

'Somewhere between midnight and dawn?'

'Got a more exact estimate?'

He shot her a wry smile and dragged his watch from the pocket where he must have put it when he'd first changed into Steve's old jeans. Someone—Frank?—had told them not to have any metal in contact with their skin, Alison vaguely remembered, because it would conduct the radiant heat. It seemed days ago, that instruction.

'My watch says five,' Nico told her.

'Five?' She shook her head, in case things were rattling

134

around inside. To her surprise, nothing was. 'Definitely, I should have asked about the Nasdaq, because…'

Shouldn't it be getting light or something? This was December, in the southern hemisphere. It should definitely be getting light, if it was five, but it didn't feel like morning yet. It felt like…the twelfth of next week.

'But that is in Italy,' Nico realised out loud. 'Sorry. Which means it is here…plus ten hours…three.'

'Three.' As meaningless as five.

'In the morning.'

'No wonder I feel…' She couldn't get out the rest of a coherent sentence.

He touched her arm and she twisted her hand and grabbed his forearm, locking the contact. He didn't try to let go, and his fingers chafed her skin. She loved the strength she could feel in the braided muscle beneath her touch.

'Steve is setting up a camp shower near the water tank, I came to tell you,' he said. 'A canvas tent, and a canvas water bag, attached to a galvanised-iron shower rose. Joan is having the men dump shovelfuls of coals in the barbecue and she's boiling cauldrons of water—she's a white witch, I'm convinced of it—so we can take turns. Short but hot.'

'A shower? Hot? I'd kill for a hot shower! There's going to be a line for it a mile long, isn't there?'

'Joan's already made a list. You're eighth and I'm ninth.'

'A list? Eighth? Better than twentieth, but who gave Joan their life savings to be first? Steve, on Jackie's behalf, I bet! And where was I when this was going on?'

'You? You were—'

'Never mind. Don't answer. I know where I was.'

'Working too hard, as you always have. Getting Lefty an airway. You did a fantastic job in there.'

'I didn't. I panicked. Then you brought me back to focus

by making me take the lead, which was…*really rotten* of you, but I'm so grateful because—'

'Because then you remembered that you can do this stuff. And you did a fantastic job,' he repeated.

'So did you. With Kim and the others.'

He ignored her. 'In the kind of conditions you've never experienced before, Alison. You should be proud of yourself. Some doctors would have been completely at sea.'

'I would have been, I think, a few years ago.' She paused for a moment. 'And I would have been tonight, without you.'

'No, there I think you're wrong. You would have got there. My pushing you speeded up the process by about twenty seconds, that's all.'

'And I'm kidding about Jackie and the shower. I know she should be first. Our firies should be first, only they're too tired to even think of it. Bit tired myself.'

'Really?'

'Just a bit.' Alison dropped his arm and slumped against the wall. Relieved of some of their weight, her legs began to shake, so she stood straight again, and felt Nico's arms around her. Didn't look at him, because her eyes seemed to have shut at some point. Her burn stung.

Really should do something about that soon, since she'd just had a little practice.

'I've seen the shower tent,' Nico said, his voice soft in her ear. 'There is room for two. We can pool our hot water allowance and get twice the time if we are prepared to share.'

'I'm 'pared to share,' she mumbled.

'I hoped you would say that.'

She felt him kiss the top of her head—mmm!—which made a new thought occur to her. 'Don't hog the water just because you're taller.'

'Don't go to sleep on my shoulder and miss out.' His voice vibrated in his chest with a low, soothing burr.

'Just a little sleep. Please?'

'Mmm, it would be nice.'

'Right here, because if I lie down I'll never get up.'

'Right here. OK.'

So they stood there in the quiet, empty corridor and leaned on each other, heads pillowed on shoulders, arms resting around warm waists, eyes closed and drowsy, scarcely moving at all for some minutes—long enough to reach the top of the shower queue. Sam came looking for them to give them the news. Like a ship's captain, he'd put himself last on the list.

Side by side, they went outside.

Joan had just taken her turn. 'I wished I didn't have to use the tent,' she said. 'Haven't showered in the open air in thirty years! But it was fabulous, every second of it.'

Wearing her own synthetic clothing again, she looked pinkly scrubbed and cheerful, but the damp towel hung over her arm was moving in an odd way, and Alison realised that the elderly woman was shaking.

Like Kim. Like Alison herself.

'You're getting very tired, Joan,' she said. 'Way too tired. You need to rest now. You haven't stopped all night.'

'I'm all right.'

'No, I don't think you are. You're running on empty, and you must find a place to lie down.'

'I rather suspect that all of those are taken!'

'We'll boot somebody onto the floor if necessary,' Nico told her, and took her arm. 'Come. You've done too much.'

'The next batch of hot water for your showers is—'

'In my hands, now,' Alison cut in firmly. 'And I can boil water with the best.'

We should have made her stop hours ago, she was thinking as she spoke. Joan's as bad as Jackie. Nico will be firm with her, thank goodness.

He was gone for a good while. Alison had time to get the water almost to boiling point, carry it over to the shower tent, pour it into the canvas bag, cool it to the right temperature with tank water and hoist it to the top of the tent, with no mishaps at any stage of the process.

A couple of folding camp chairs had been set up outside the tent to hold clothing and towels and a gas-lamp. She stripped inside the tent and reached out again to put the discarded garments on one chair's fabric seat, using them to protect the stethoscope that still seemed so precious to her.

'Are we still going with pooling our water?' said Nico's voice.

'That, or you can just sell me your share. I'll pay three times the market rate, in US currency,' she called back, grinning. Her heart lifted just because he was here and at last they were alone.

Alone, and thrumming with an expectancy that made her tingle all over.

'My share is not for sale at any price,' he told her.

'Then we'll have to pool.' Her voice came out breathless, and the casual veneer was onion-skin thin when she asked, 'How's Joan?'

'Lying on a fold-out bed in the old house. Asleep, I hope. I'm a little concerned. She's sounding short of breath now. We'll check her through until morning.'

'We'll check everyone. But for now…'

'For now, let's not think like doctors,' Nico agreed.

A few seconds later, he slipped through the vertical slit in the shower tent, his naked body contoured with shadow in the dim light which the gas-lamp threw onto the side of the tent. For just a few seconds Alison felt self-conscious, and a little nervous, but then she forgot any of that in her overwhelming reaction to his presence.

He was gorgeous, and so perfectly made. Not an ounce of fat, nothing but satiny, olive-toned skin, contoured muscle and strong bone. Her breath caught in her throat and she didn't try to hide the way her eyes roved over him with hunger and greed. Her hands hung at the sides of her body, tingling with her readiness to touch him.

'So long since I've seen you like this,' he whispered.

'My body's changed…'

'Not so much.' His eyes were very dark in the soft light, but she had no doubt as to where they were focused. 'A little riper, that's all, and it suits you. You are so beautiful, Alison.'

'You are, too. You make me ache.'

She touched her hands to his shoulders and he held her close. In the dark nest at his groin, she felt the stirring of his arousal, fully matched by her own heat. Needing to taste him, she printed her lips on his bare skin—neck, jaw, chest. She felt the rise and fall of his controlled breathing against her mouth, and shivered with awareness.

'Cold?' he asked.

'Not with you here.'

He dipped his head towards the ridge of her collar-bone and kissed her, and she felt the tiny sting of moisture from his tongue. 'I can taste the smoke on your skin. Let's wash it off.'

He reached up and opened the screw-in shower rose, releasing the cascade of hot water down onto them. As they held each other, it pooled between them, ran down their thighs, blanketed their shoulders. When they were soaked, Nico turned the water off again, because even with a second bucket waiting just outside the tent, it wouldn't last long.

Earlier, Jackie had stuck a cake of soap onto a nail protruding from one of the shower tent's angled poles. Nico lathered it onto his hands and began to soap Alison's body, running the wet white film over her breasts and stomach and buttocks and thighs until she was aware of every inch of her own clean skin.

'Give me some, too,' she said, and he wiped his soapy palms against hers, letting their fingers tangle together until she pulled them away with a laugh. 'No, I want to wash you. All over.'

She lathered his back and his neck and his shoulders, her touch possessive and exploring, every fingertip eager for more.

Soon their bodies were slick and slippery with fragrant lather and they were both laughing. Because it felt good. Because it was past three o'clock in the morning, and the wind had gone and no more living embers fell from the sky. Because they were alive, and so, miraculously, was everyone else.

Nico lowered the shower bag, poured in the final bucket of water, raised the pulley and released the flow again, so that it chased the rose-scented soap down their bodies. After hours of pores clogged with sweat and dirt and smoke, Alison's skin felt as new as a baby's and every bit as sensitive.

They rinsed each other, then Nico kissed her until the water supply ran out. It was such a warm night, and heat still radiated towards them from the concrete water tank nearby. Neither of them felt cold.

'Who's number ten for the shower?' Alison whispered.

'Deirdre, but she was fast asleep last time I looked,' Nico whispered back. 'Sam has crashed, too. I'm not sure if anyone else is still awake but Frank and Steve. They want to keep watch for embers, even without the wind. But I doubt they'll patrol much around here, there's so little fuel to catch alight.'

'So no one's going to come and…'

'No.' His mouth brushed hers. 'No one is going to interrupt us. This could be the most private place around.'

Can we?

Could we?

He didn't ask, and she didn't answer. He just kept kissing her, soft and lazy at first, then with increasing depth and heat. Until their skin dried. Until her body went as soft as melted chocolate. Until she could hardly tell which way was up, and where the boundaries between their two bodies were.

She tried to kiss him back but he shook his head and whispered, 'No, not yet. My turn.' So she surrendered completely, closing her eyes and letting herself ride the slow, swelling tide that came from deep inside her as he lavished his touch on her body.

She hadn't forgotten what a wonderful lover he was, but still every moment of it felt new. Cupping her breasts, he abraded their peaked crests with his mouth until her breathing was ragged and out of control. She dug her fingers into his shoulders and ran them through his hair, flooded with a wild current of sensation as he went lower.

Finally, he let her use her own mouth the way he'd used his—to taste and explore and drive him wild. Every kiss she gave him was an act of claiming and rediscovery. Wouldn't there be a way in which he would always be hers, for the rest of their lives, because of this night? She had to believe it, because this was so intense that nothing else would have made any sense, nothing else counted at all. She had one brief thought about protection, about the risk, but it was minimal at this point in her cycle and in any case she didn't care. She honestly didn't. She'd welcome whatever came.

He made completely sure she was ready before taking their intimacy to the next level, finding her swollen heat and showing the satisfaction he felt in a deep sound of expectancy.

'Please,' she begged him, almost sobbing. 'Yes. Don't wait.'

'Put your arms around my neck,' he whispered. 'Don't let go.'

'I don't ever want to let you go.'

'That's right…'

He lifted her against him, her thighs spread against his hips, and she trusted his strength so utterly that she let her back arch and her head relax as he manoeuvred to fill her. 'Oh, yes, Nico…'

She clung close to him, her legs locking them both in place and the rocking of his hips against her opened body for long, delectable minutes bringing her to the very edge over and over, until a final powerful thrust sent them both over it, their release a cascade of pure sensation that had her panting and gasping and calling his name.

Even when it was over, she didn't want to come back to earth. Easing her legs to the ground, she stayed in the tight, hard circle of his arms, feeling safe and blessed and so happy. Yesterday, seven years ago, tomorrow, the rest of her life—none of it counted for anything.

Today was all that mattered.

Now.

This.

'Say something,' he growled finally, after they'd stayed motionless in each other's arms for minutes on end.

'Can't. Don't want to. Don't make me put any of this into words.'

He laughed and pressed his warm face into her neck. 'May I say something?'

'Careful that it doesn't break the spell,' she whispered.

She couldn't have explained what she meant, but he seemed to understand. 'Would the spell break if I told you how perfect this was?'

'Is,' she corrected. 'It's still perfect.'

'How perfect it is,' he repeated obediently.

'No. I guess you can say that.'

'It's perfect, Alison. Utterly perfect.'

He kissed her lightly on the knob of her shoulder, in the curve of her neck, all sorts of places. They were kisses that made promises.

I trust you.

This isn't over.

I'll be here in the morning.

Alison believed the promises but she couldn't see how he'd be able to keep them. How either of them would be able to. She was supposed to fly up to Byron Bay in about…oh, ten hours. In some ways it seemed like half a lifetime, in others just the blink of an eye.

'When do you leave Australia?' she asked him, dreading the answer so much that she could hardly get out the question.

'Tomorrow…no, today,' he said, confirming her fears. 'I have an evening flight out of Sydney. But I imagine there'll be some rescheduling going on and it'll be Monday instead, because it doesn't seem possible that I'll make it tonight.'

'No.'

She didn't say, 'I hope you won't,' but she thought it…and then realised how crazy that was. As if an extra day would make a difference! The best they'd achieved tonight had been to understand the mistakes they'd made seven years ago. This wasn't a new beginning, just a clearer and more satisfying line drawn at the bottom of the page.

'Do you believe what I told you earlier?' she whispered,

scared about what he might say. 'Do you believe that I didn't want your money and your connections seven years ago? That I was more afraid of those things than anything else?'

'I believe that,' he answered. 'The only reason I got it wrong before, the only reason I saw it through my father's eyes, was because we were both too young and too unsure of ourselves in certain ways to understand what was really going on.'

'Then I'm very glad we got another chance to work out the truth.'

It was better than nothing after all.

'So am I.'

Nico's arms tightened around her again, and Alison wondered how she would ever manage to let him go. She'd have to, soon, if either of them was going to get a chance at sleep in the hour or two of night that still remained. Suddenly, the bone-deep weariness that had been lying in wait for her for hours—months?—swept over her, dragging both her body and her spirits down.

'I must get dressed…check on everyone…get some sleep,' she said. 'It'll be starting to get light soon, won't it?'

'Learn to delegate, Alison,' he teased her gently. 'We'll both get dressed, I'll check our patients and you can get the sleep.'

'You're not going to?'

'The fatigue hasn't hit me again yet, but I can feel that it's hit you. I'm holding you up, the way I was in the corridor an hour ago.'

'Sorry. I'm sorry.' She sagged even more deeply against him, feeling that she'd almost lose consciousness if he let her go now.

'Am I asking for an apology?' he whispered.

She laughed, took a couple of deep, strengthening breaths.

She had to do this herself, she couldn't wait for him. She had to be the one to make the move.

OK. Just do it, Alison. Just make it happen.

Another breath, then she successfully eased herself away and reached out of the tent for her clothes. Her own clothes, not Jackie's filthy, fire-stained ones. In an odd way, she would have preferred to put those back on. Nico had touched them as they'd clung together during the fire-storm. Their texture and their smell would forever remind her of that searing interval. They didn't seem like someone else's garments any more, but like a memento of the most vital minutes of her life.

Thinking this as she dragged her shorts up her legs, she winced and hissed in a breath. She'd forgotten about the still untreated burn. It would be clean now, at least. Maybe that was all it really needed.

But Nico had heard the hissing sound. 'What's wrong?'

She shrugged, playing it down. 'I got a burn on the back of my leg at some point, that's all. While I was racing round with a wet blanket. Hours ago. I don't even remember it happening.'

'And you haven't treated it, right?'

She laughed and shrugged again, admitting guilt.

He made a click with his teeth, but didn't say anything.

'So, am I going to get into trouble for that?' she asked after a moment.

'You may have to put up with a rather impatient medical professional at this point. I'll take a look at it when we get to the house, but I'm not promising to be gentle!'

He was, of course. As gentle as he would have been towards a child. They found a makeshift and unoccupied bed set up on an ancient couch in the old part of the house. Someone had tucked in clean sheets and covered one of the throw pillows in a smooth white pillowcase.

'Yours,' Nico told her quietly, because Midori, Deirdre and Joan were sleeping nearby. 'Now, roll onto your stomach, let go of that security blanket of yours and I'll get to work.'

Alison surrendered her stethoscope to him and heard a faint sound as he pushed it into his pocket, then the tearing of a packet. A moment later, she felt a cool gel covering the area of blistered skin.

'You should have done something about this before,' he muttered. 'It's as big as the palm of my hand. I can't believe you're still just as bad at taking care of yourself as you ever were. You know what you need?'

'No...' she mumbled. 'Tell me what I need.'

Nico sighed between his teeth. 'Forget it. All we both need right now is to rest.'

At any other time she might have pushed him to say what was on his mind, but maybe they'd both sensed that this wasn't the setting in which they needed to talk. She let it go, and the exhaustion came flooding back.

Nico used the same clingfilm he'd applied to Kim's hand and several of the firies' burns. Since it was the contact of the burned skin's raw nerve-endings with the air that caused so much pain with burns, the fine, impermeable plastic provided pain relief as well as protection against infection.

Nico's touch was soft, economical and sure, and when his warm fingers rested on the uninjured skin higher on her calf, thrills of need and awareness chased each other all the way up her legs and spine. Alison wanted him in her arms so badly. She didn't think she could have made love again tonight, explosive though it had been. She was just too exhausted now. But to hold him, to feel his breathing deepen against her chest, to surround herself in his warmth and his male scent...

'There,' he whispered, and it was the last thing she heard

before sleep floated her away. When he eased his body next to hers a little later, after checking on their sleeping patients, she didn't even stir.

Less than an hour later, three-quarters asleep, Nico fought his awareness of dawn. Couldn't be getting light yet. That would be too cruel. He'd only been lying here for a few minutes, it seemed.

Lying here next to Alison.

She was deeply asleep, her body warm and relaxed and still, apart from the slow, undulating movement of her breathing. Rising further from sleep, Nico could smell the rose scent of the shower soap on her skin. The couch was narrow and they were lying very close, wrapped together. He didn't have to move more than an inch to bring his face against her loosely tangled hair.

Ah.

It smelt so sweet, *her* smell and no one else's.

Dawn came early in December, in this part of the world, but still he had two or three hours more, didn't he, before he had to think about the rest of his life? Two or three hours just to lie here like this, in the delicious suspension between wakefulness and sleep, aware enough to feel Alison's body against his from calf to forehead, sleepy enough to melt against her in total relaxation.

No.

Of course he didn't.

It was already two hours since he and Alison had left Mark keeping watch over the injured firefighters. He knew that the former nurse would have alerted them to any emergency, and he'd done a brief check of his own, but that wasn't good enough. It should be the other man's turn for some rest now. With a reluctance that raged in his body like an aching fever, Nico eased away from Alison, taking her scent with him on his clothing and skin.

She still didn't stir.

As he stretched, he looked down at her and his stomach gave a painful lurch. This time yesterday he'd had no idea that he had the capacity to feel like this. And what about tomorrow? Would he be able to trust anything about this overwhelming experience once his life resumed its normal course?

He felt totally at sea, awed by a connection that could survive so many years of distance, touched to the depths by how much he still yearned to take care of her, daunted by how different their lives were, and too rational to believe that there was an easy answer. Instinctively, he wanted more time, more clues, less fatigue and drama clouding his judgement, but he knew that none of it was going to happen.

As they'd done with the medical treatment they'd given, both he and Alison would have to make do with what was at hand.

CHAPTER TEN

AT THE corner of his vision Nico glimpsed a movement and turned away from the precious sight of Alison in sleep to discover Steve entering the room. The man didn't waste words.

'Jackie's in labour,' he said. 'Don't suppose that's going to surprise you very much, right?'

'I think we've all had an inkling that it might happen,' Nico answered. He clapped a hand on Steve's back. 'How is she feeling?'

'Good, but she's nauseous and she's not sure if that's right. Can you come and check things out? Sorry if I woke you up.'

'You didn't. I'd better wake Alison up also, because we have other people who need monitoring.'

'Thanks,' Steve said. 'Jackie's pretty annoyed at the baby right now.'

'If the baby is as determined as your wife…'

'I know!'

They grimaced at each other, then both laughed wryly. Nico stepped back to the couch and rested his hand on Alison's shoulder. She didn't react, so he pressed a little harder, then caressed the graceful bone structure in its covering of soft skin and cotton cloth. She made a sound of sleepy protest, and when he shook her gently and softly said her name, her eyes dragged open.

'Wh—?'

'We're needed.'

'Lefty—'

'No, Jackie's having the baby,' Steve told her.

'*Having* it? Like, before breakfast?'

'She thinks so,' Steve said. 'She was having contractions for hours before she told me.'

'Before she told any of us!'

'They were pretty mild, but they stepped up a couple of hours ago and we've been timing them and we both think it's close.'

'Where is she, Steve?' Alison asked, sitting up. She looked stiff-limbed and bleary-eyed and beautiful, with her red-gold beacon of hair a fine mess all around her face, and her eyelids creased with inadequate sleep.

'On a camp stretcher on the kitchen floor,' Steve answered. 'Pretty much everywhere else is taken. She's fine, apart from feeling queasy and a bit shaky.'

'That might be the effect of smoke inhalation,' Alison said. 'Give me my stethoscope, I'll check her breathing.'

Nico didn't challenge her possessive attitude to the piece of medical equipment that was so important to her, he simply reached into his pocket and handed it across, while saying, 'The labour itself, though, Steve. Have her waters broken?'

'Not yet. Everything's pretty steady and quiet. It's been nice. We've been talking until the last hour when the contractions started getting a bit relentless. I wondered if we should try to move her, but she doesn't want to.'

'No, best not, if the birth is close,' Alison agreed. 'Don't you think, Nico?' She slung the stethoscope around her neck and clutched its rubber tubing against her heart, making Nico smile to himself. Steve went ahead of them, and she added in a low tone, 'So, did that sound as if I knew what I was talking about?'

He laced his fingers through hers and gave a soft laugh. 'Are you claiming you don't?'

'I haven't delivered a baby in more than seven years. You have to be able to trump me on this one, Nico! Sierra Leone?'

'Yes, lots of them, and mostly in conditions far more primitive than this.'

'Were you good at it? Tell me you were!'

He laughed again. 'The mothers were. And Jackie will be. We've all seen how tough she is.'

'OK, so the baby's yours.' She didn't try to hide her relief, and grinned when he planted a kiss on her neck.

'The baby is mine? Word that a little more tactfully next time, if Steve is listening,' he told her softly.

'Point taken. The baby is Steve's, and Jackie has to do the work. I'll take a look at Lefty and Kim and the others, see how Mark is holding up and tell him he may have to wait a little longer to get some sleep. If no one else is awake—Jerry, Sarah, Eddie, Joan—I'm not going to disturb them now.'

Leaving Nico for the moment—it shouldn't feel like such a wrench, but it did—Alison moved quickly and quietly through rooms that now seemed very familiar, finding that everyone seemed peacefully asleep or at least happy to rest with their eyes closed. Only Frank still prowled around, having snatched a couple of hours' sleep earlier, he told her.

'You're going to be a grandfather pretty soon, according to your son.'

'Seems so. Unbelievable night!'

'Yes.'

In a strange, unsettling way she didn't want it to end. Temporarily, the farmhouse had become the boundary of her whole world. Hers and Nico's. A world in which they'd miraculously connected again, with emotion and drama pushed to breaking point all around them, even while they knew it couldn't last.

When Alison reached the main bedroom where the fire-fighters were, she said quietly to Mark, 'I'm sorry, we were hoping to relieve your watch, but we've got a baby on the way in the kitchen. Can you stay awake a little longer?'

'Couldn't sleep if I tried. I'm still pretty twitchy. Kim's restless. I think the painkiller has worn off.'

'It would have. It wasn't as strong as she really needed. Let me take a look at Lefty.'

'I took his obs a few minutes ago. Respiration still shallow and fast, pulse too high, blood pressure too low. He's OK, but what he really needs are drugs that we haven't got, and hospital treatment. That pen arrangement isn't sterile, for a start.'

One of the other men stirred and sat up. Apparently he'd heard most of their conversation. 'We need to get on the radio,' he said. 'Find out the status of the fire and the road. You want an ambulance up here as soon as it can get through, don't you, Doctor?'

'I'd just about sell my soul for an ambulance, yes! A helicopter evacuation, for preference.'

'I'll see what I can find out.' He struggled to his feet. 'There must be some better news by now.'

Alison confirmed Mark's sense that Lefty's condition was stable for the moment, then she went down the corridor to the kitchen, where she found Jackie in the grip of a powerful contraction. When it ebbed, she panted, 'I'd be OK if I could breathe better. My lungs feel horrible.'

'I know, Jackie,' Nico said. 'There's not a lot we can do, but the baby's still moving and it will be safely out soon.'

Over Steve's and Jackie's heads, Alison met Nico's eyes and saw that he was more concerned than he was letting on.

'Let me check the heartbeat, Jackie,' she said.

Putting the earpieces of the stethoscope in place, she pressed the metal disc to Jackie's abdomen and listened, holding her breath and waiting for the strong heartbeat she so badly wanted to hear.

The heartbeat was definitely there. She could distinguish it from Jackie's own, and it was faster than an adult's, as that of a baby *in utero* should be, but it wasn't as good as she would have liked. Nico's suspicions were correct. This baby was showing signs of distress.

'Waters?' she mouthed to Nico. The quilt beneath Jackie's body seemed dry, and he confirmed with a shake of his head that they hadn't yet broken.

'I'll do it now,' he said. She knew he could tell by her reaction that the heartbeat wasn't as strong as they would both have liked.

'Is everything OK?' Jackie asked, her voice high. A contraction gripped her once more.

'Looking good,' Nico answered. 'But we do want to get the baby out soon.'

Unable to speak through the contraction, Jackie gasped as soon as it was over, 'So do I!'

'It won't be long, once I've broken your waters,' he predicted, although it didn't always work that way.

The painless action of rupturing the membrane should speed up labour and get the baby out quicker. It might also reveal more about the baby's state, and Alison didn't need any recent obstetric experience to know that if the waters were stained with meconium, they'd have to take particular care on delivery.

They didn't have the right instrument available, of course. Nico had reboiled some of the unused water heated earlier for showers and had sterilised several makeshift kitchen items, including a metal skewer and a basting bulb. Now Alison watched as he padded towels beneath Jackie's thighs, then held the skewer and slid his hand carefully beneath the sheet he'd draped over her body.

Seconds later, there came a flood of meconium-stained liquid. With the pressure of the baby's head on the fluid-filled amniotic sac, he'd barely brushed the membrane with the skewer's blunt point before it had ruptured. Jackie would have felt nothing more than the gush of warm fluid.

'Towels, Alison,' he said.

She was already right beside him, whisking away the soaked towels and wadding more into place. Another strong contraction came, and Jackie moaned and shuddered.

'Jackie, I'd like to check your dilatation—can we do that? Say no if you want.'

'It's OK,' she panted.

Nico placed one hand on her abdomen while the other measured the opened and effaced cervix. 'One tiny bit left to fold back,' he said. 'And it's paper thin. This is great, Jackie. This is what we want.'

Another contraction. Jackie dragged at Steve's hand, and he frowned. He'd probably detected a little more cause for concern than Nico and Alison had admitted to out loud. No sense in getting Jackie anxious when she had so much to deal with already.

'When you need to push, tell us,' Nico said. 'And if you want to change position. You're calling the shots, Jackie. You're almost ready, and the baby is nice and low. It won't be long now.'

Another contraction nudged hard against the ebb of the previous one, and Jackie lost control, sobbing and moaning. 'It's horrible.' With the next one, she gave an animal grunt and said urgently, 'Push! Can I?'

'Do you want to change position, Jackie?' Nico asked her quickly.

'No. Can't.'

'Steve, stand behind her shoulders, support her if she

wants to lift her head. Jackie, draw your thighs up and grip onto them as you bear down.'

'Unhh!'

'Alison, I'm going to need you for suction and cleaning.' Before the baby took its first breath, she knew, because if any of that thick, sticky meconium got into the delicate new lungs, a fatal infection could take hold. She'd need to do a finger sweep of its little mouth with a freshly gloved hand, and then she'd use that handy basting bulb…

With the next contraction, Jackie began to push. The head crowned nicely, but slipped back when the contraction was over. She pushed again, with the same result, and with a fresh surge of the stained liquid which had both Nico and Alison increasingly concerned.

'I'm too tired for this,' Jackie moaned, in the five-second interval between the relentless contractions.

Her push was less powerful this time.

'Jackie, you're doing very well,' Nico said, his accent stronger than usual. 'But you need to do better. We want to get the baby out soon. We need to.'

'Why?' They could all hear the new alarm in her voice. It turned to another grunt of effort as she began to bear down again.

'You've been so strong these past twenty-four hours so I'm going to be honest. The baby's heartbeat has slowed down and we don't want to make it harder on the little one with a prolonged delivery—'

'Unh!' Her whole body seemed to surge with new strength and determination as soon as she heard the words.

'And the staining of your waters is also a sign of distress. The head is crowning but it's slipping—' He broke off. 'Push, yes, that's good. That's much better. Now, breathe and push again, yes.'

The contraction ebbed and she gasped out, 'Higher, Steve. Hold me higher.'

'Keep the pressure, Jackie, yes.'

'This is really good now,' Alison added. 'The head is coming.'

Jackie's body shook with the force of her effort, and blood darkened almost to purple in her face. As the contraction eased, she began to prepare at once for the next onslaught and when it came, the head was born, slipping round to face sideways as it came.

'Now pant, Jackie, don't push. You must not push with this next contraction.'

Jackie managed to nod, although her eyes looked wild and panicky. Steve was gulping out dry sobs beside her, massaging her hand to bruising point, spilling out the occasional stammering word of love and encouragement.

With eyes closed and a coating of waxy vernix, the baby's face looked still and lifeless, which was exactly how Alison wanted it. Also, there was no cord around the neck, which took away a second source of delay. Working as fast as she could, she wiped around the lips and nose, ran her gloved finger around the inside of the mouth and suctioned out both nostrils and the baby's mouth with her makeshift instrument.

'Clear?' Nico barked.

'Yes!'

Jackie's panting was frantic. In the grip of another contraction, she desperately wanted to push. 'No, Jackie!' Nico told her. He checked the baby's airway, confirming Alison's opinion and at last told his patient, 'OK, again, now.'

A yell wrenched its way from Jackie's body as she bore down with a mighty effort. Nico delivered the anterior shoulder, and the second shoulder slipped free with ease. He cupped his hands gently around the baby's chest and seconds later it was fully born. 'It's a girl!' he said, and cradled the little body in a thick pad of towel.

She breathed at once and began to cry, but the sound wasn't as lusty and strong as Nico wanted. He massaged her little chest, while pink slowly radiated outwards. Much better! Alison dried the tiny body, then Nico gently lifted her across Jackie's stomach and into her arms. 'Around 3500 grams, I'd guess, Jackie. That's a great, healthy size.'

'Oh! Oh! Oh!' was all the new mother could say.

Alison's gaze met Nico's and her eyes filled with tears. They smiled at each other, lost for some seconds in a shared moment that felt almost as special as what had happened to Jackie and Steve. Alison wondered about her friends Mike and Charlotte—whether they'd had their baby, whether things had gone well, whether they'd had a girl and called her Topaz. Sydney was only a few hours away, but right now it seemed like part of another world.

'Beautiful,' Nico murmured.

'Yes. We hoped this wouldn't happen here, but now that it has, it almost seems right.'

'It does.' And their part in it wasn't over yet.

Jackie didn't even notice Nico tying the cord with water-sterilised kitchen string at ten, fifteen and twenty centimetres from the baby's navel, and examining the small tear Jackie had sustained. They had no equipment for suturing it, but many medical professionals believed that a tear of that size would heal better on its own, Alison knew.

'She's beautiful,' Steve whispered. He kissed his wife and beamed down at the baby.

'Would you like to try putting her to the breast, Jackie?' Nico suggested.

'Can I?'

'Definitely.'

The cord was long, and he wouldn't be in any hurry to

cut it in an environment like this, where infection could be a threat and excess bleeding a life-endangering emergency. He'd want the afterbirth safely delivered, however, and the baby's sucking would stimulate the contraction of the uterus.

Wishing her obstetric skills weren't so rusty, Alison helped Jackie to get her baby into the right position, her head angled towards the swollen breast and her lower lip rolled out.

'Oh, she knows exactly what to do!' Jackie exclaimed in amazement. 'Oh, you darling girl!' The baby's tiny bud-like mouth had closed over a darkened nipple just as it should, beyond the hardened peak and against the areola. Jackie and Steve watched, and laughed, and cried.

'Does she have a name, Jackie?' Alison asked.

Steve and Jackie looked at each other. 'Um…'

'You see, for some reason we were sure she was a boy,' Steve said.

'What was your boy's name?'

'Lindsay John.'

'I've heard Lindsay used for a girl,' Alison said. 'Lindsay Jane?'

The new parents looked at each other again. 'I like it,' Jackie said.

'So do I.'

Suddenly, all four of them were laughing. 'Well, that was easy… Oh, here comes a contraction…'

'It'll be mild, Jackie. The placenta has come away and is ready to be delivered.' Nico focused his attention once more, and the final stage was soon completed. He cut the cord between the second and third tie, and covered it in gauze, then checked little Lindsay thoroughly, wrapped in her towel blanket and snuggled her close against her mother again.

People had started to stir and move about. It was almost seven.

'I'm taking up the space that everyone's going to want,' Jackie realised. 'The kitchen. How did we end up like this?'

Alison met Nico's eyes again.

How *did* they end up like this?

It felt so special and magical that she couldn't think straight, couldn't smell the smoke any more, couldn't think about patients and radio contact and road closures and ambulances and travel. She tried to imagine saying goodbye to Nico, and couldn't do that either. Just couldn't picture it at all.

Would they swap telephone numbers and e-mail addresses?

Make promises?

Tell lies?

'Steve, we'll each take one end of the camp stretcher and carry these two somewhere a little more private, shall we?' Nico suggested.

'If the road is open, should I go to hospital at some point?' Jackie asked.

'I'd like you to, Jackie, and the baby of course. Just to be on the safe side. She looks beautiful—in my head I gave her an Apgar score of eight, which is close to perfect—and I'll examine her more thoroughly soon, but with that colour and the way she's so eager to feed, she's already getting protection from your antibodies.'

'You were worried for a while, both of you.'

'Yes. Things could have been different if you hadn't delivered so quickly.'

'Yep, I got that. There was a reason why I stopped wimping out on my pushing.' She gave a tired laugh as Nico and Steve bent their legs and hauled her and baby Lindsay up.

'Jackie, you are one of the least wimpy people I've ever met!' Alison said.

'Put you across in the old house?' Nico suggested. 'Where Joan and Deirdre and Midori are sleeping?'

Were sleeping.

Deirdre and Midori were already up, while Joan lay in bed, awake but quiet. She still looked very tired, but when she saw Jackie and the new baby, she laughed in delight. 'Oh, good heavens! The things you miss out on when you snatch a nap!'

'Snatch another one, and keep Jackie company,' Alison suggested.

'No, must help with breakfast,' Joan answered briskly, then hopped off her couch and began to neaten the clothing she'd slept in.

'Will you get the bassinet from our room, Steve?' Jackie asked. 'I want her with me for now, but if I need to put her down…'

'Yep,' he said. 'Someone's covered it in plastic, which was nice. It'll be clean.'

'Nothing is clean,' she answered. 'We're just so used to the smoke we can't smell it any more.'

'I'll relieve Mark,' Nico said quietly to Alison, 'and check on everyone else. Jackie would prefer a woman to help her get comfortable, I'm sure.'

'Yes, she may want a wash, and some help in the bathroom.'

The two of them spent a half-hour together. Putting Lindsay Jane in her bassinet, Alison assisted Jackie with a sponge bath, and encouraged her when she discovered that her groin was still too swollen from the birth to allow her bladder to empty. 'Just relax. We'll have another try in ten minutes or so.' This next attempt was successful, which came as a relief.

'I'm starving!' Jackie said.

'Let me see what I can find.'

Alison found Joan, with her usual ambitious plans about cooking, and told her firmly, 'No. You're not doing eggs and bacon for twenty-odd people, when we still don't have power in the house.'

'Scrambled eggs,' Joan said. 'Outside. Easy.'

'Joan, no!'

But Joan was already foraging in a cupboard, as if she'd worked in this kitchen for years. 'There's a real old-fashioned cast-iron pan in here that would be perfect for—'

She stopped suddenly, with her body bending into the cupboard and the pan's big black handle already grasped in her hand.

'For scrambled eggs,' she finished.

'Joan?'

'I've pulled a muscle or something. I'm all right.' She straightened, with the heavy pan in her hand, but seconds later it dangled then dropped, clattering on the wooden floor with a bell-like sound. 'I'm all right,' she repeated. 'My arm hurts. And my neck. Burning.'

She pressed a fist between her left shoulder and her collar-bone and massaged the area roughly, while Alison watched in dawning horror. Joan had turned grey, and her face was filmed with sweat and twisted with pain. She appeared to be in full cardiac arrest.

Alison reached her just in time, and held the sagging body in her arms with her own heart pounding and her mind racing, close to tears. Joan had been such a heroine. Alison felt as if they'd known each other for years. This couldn't be happening. Not to dear Joan! Not now!

We have a dozen other people in need of better medical care than we can give.

We're forty-five minutes from the nearest hospital, with no working vehicle and the road still apparently closed.

Some kind of med-evac helicopter flight? Emergency services in the area are stretched so thin they've already snapped. By the time it could get here…

We have the defibrillator.

The one piece of good news was the last to penetrate her awareness. She hadn't thought about it since Nico had brought it in from the crippled fire truck several hours ago.

Lowering Joan's inert body to the floor, which was still protected by the plastic sheet that Nico had laid on it as Jackie had approached delivery, Alison prayed for some sign that Joan's heart was beating after all. 'Come on, Joanie, don't do this now! Come on, I can't bear it, you're such a fighter!'

But the elderly woman gave no sign of awareness or movement. Whipping her precious stethoscope into position, Alison listened for breathing sounds and heartbeat and could find nothing. Instinctively, her index and middle fingers came to rest on Joan's neck and the absence of a carotid artery pulse confirmed her worse fear. This was definitely a full arrest.

'Nico!' she almost screamed. 'Someone! In the kitchen, now!'

She didn't wait for a response, but began CPR immediately, knowing that her physical capacity to keep it up at the required level of strength and speed for more than a few minutes would be severely compromised by the fatiguing events of the previous sixteen hours. A hundred compressions a minute, ideally, punctuated by two breaths for every fifteen compressions. For anyone, it was exhausting work.

'Come on, Joan, sweetheart!' she whispered harshly, then raised her voice and yelled again. 'Nico! Anyone! Now!' The words jerked out of her as she pumped Joan's chest.

Someone must have heard her. Someone would come.

Nico did, when she was already feeling a burning fatigue in her arms, shoulders and stomach muscles. 'Oh, lord, no! She's arrested?'

'Yes. No pulse. It happened so *fast*!' She panted as she spoke. 'Where's the defibrillator?'

'Bathroom bench-top. Get it while I take over. Let's hope it's an up-to-date model.'

She didn't argue, knowing how much more effective his strength would be. Racing down the corridor, she found a couple more people on their way to the kitchen, having re-acted to the urgency in her tone. She hardly took in who they were. 'Joan's had a heart attack. Thank God for the defibrillator from the ambulance!'

'Need more help?'

'Find Mark!'

Alison was back in the kitchen within a minute, to find Nico's strong body aggressively at work. 'Any response?'

'Not yet. Get her set up while I keep going.'

It wasn't easy. Working around his rhythmic movement, Alison unfastened Joan's now-crumpled blouse and bra. No jewellery. No pacemaker scar. Chest still clammy. She grabbed one of the few remaining towels that they hadn't needed during Jackie's delivery and wiped the area dry, her fingertips crushed more than once by the heels of Nico's hand.

OK, now, the machine itself. Basically familiar, but not an exact twin of the types she'd encountered before. Better than she'd expected, to be honest. Better than she'd feared. The local community must have had a recent fundraising drive to purchase an expensive piece of equipment like this. It had a visible ECG screen, a blood-pressure cuff and a finger probe that in hindsight could have been used to give them a more accurate gauge of Lefty's and Kim's conditions.

Nico glanced at it and shook his head. 'Can't help. Just work it out fast. I'm not getting anything here.'

Joan looked even greyer than before, and horribly *absent* somehow. Alison knew that everyone at the Porters' farm would unequivocally want her back.

She made a quick assessment of the equipment. OK, it was the type that analysed the heart rhythm automatically, which cut out one step in the process. She attached the cables to the defibrillator pads, and the pads to Joan's chest. Nico stopped his steady, powerful pumping and breathing and they stood back, both making a last-minute check for hazards. No metal in contact with Joan's body. No water nearby.

Pressing a key, Alison got a read-out on the machine which confirmed that Joan's heart was producing a shockable rhythm.

'Ready?' Nico said.

'Yes. Shocking her now.' She pressed the shock key, and Joan's inert body jolted, but her heart's electrical activity remained disorganised and ineffective. 'We'll go again,' Alison said, and the machine delivered a second jolt, while both she and Nico held their breath.

'Yes!' Nico exclaimed a moment later, and scrambled close to Joan again, to work on her breathing.

Mark entered the room. 'I heard.'

'We have a pulse… We have her breathing,' Nico said.

'Do we have her conscious?'

'Not yet. Flutter, maybe.'

'What drugs do we have from the ambulance?'

'Aspirin, atropine, some new ligocaine equivalent—only you don't call it ligocaine, do you? And the Australian name of the new thing I can't remember either…'

'The road is open for emergency vehicles,' Mark told them. 'And we've been told we can get a helicopter in about an hour and fifteen minutes, if we need one.'

Nico gave a weary laugh. 'I wouldn't want to be selfish here, but I'd say that with a patient five minutes out of full cardiac arrest, another with an emergency cricothyroidotomy in place and a firefighter with serious burns, not to mention a mother with a newborn, yes, we'll take the helicopter. Preferably two.'

'Do you hear that, Joan?' Alison whispered. 'You're going to be airlifted out of here, to somewhere you'll really be taken care of.'

When she raised her head to look at Nico, the tears in her eyes blurred her vision so much that she had to blink several times before she saw the tears in his.

CHAPTER ELEVEN

'THE tour company is sending a mini-bus for us,' Sam told Alison wearily. 'It should be here in about an hour.'

The chopping vibration of helicopter blades threatened to drown his last few words. The machine had been circling overhead for the past few minutes, in search of the best place to land, as close to the house as possible. There would be qualified personnel aboard, Alison knew, with all the right equipment. They would charge into the house in their overalls and helmets with their big, impressive kits on their backs. Joan, Lefty and Kim would all be airlifted to the nearest major hospital, and the responsibility she'd shared with Nico and Mark would be over.

For Joan, in particular, the evacuation couldn't come soon enough. She'd regained consciousness but was confused, restless, too feeble to talk and she was in pain. Nico admitted he'd probably fractured a rib or two during CPR. It wouldn't be unusual with an elderly patient like this.

Alison hadn't left Joan's side in the past hour, alarmed by the salvos of big, spiky ectopic beats showing on the ECG screen. She and Nico had given three doses of atropine at one-minute intervals, holding their breath because some patients' hearts speeded up so much and so suddenly with this treatment that they went straight back into ventribular fibrillation and full arrest.

They couldn't lose Joan. They just couldn't.

'Let me go and tell the others about the new bus,' Sam added, and almost bumped into Troy on the way out of the kitchen. 'What's this, mate?'

'Breakfast, courtesy of a couple of burning logs,' Troy said, and held out a plate of scrambled eggs on toast and a mug of instant coffee to Alison. 'Sorry it's been such a long time coming.'

'Oh, please!' she answered. 'I'm impressed that it's here at all.'

'Heard the news about the mini-bus on its way,' Troy said to Sam. 'Sarah and I will be the first on board, let me tell you! That's if we can fight our way ahead of Jerry and bloody Valda! Time to open the champagne from yesterday's picnic, do you think?'

'I'd take a glass,' Alison admitted.

'If I can find where it got put. And I'm supposed to report to both of you that there are two Rural Fire Service four-wheel-drives on the way as well, which'll be able to take some of the firies to the local hospital for treatment.'

'Right.' Sam nodded, as he left.

'Steve, Jackie and the baby will hitch a ride with them,' Troy continued to Alison, 'and Nico is going, too, so he can hand over to the hospital staff. ''Inability to delegate'' he called it, but Steve looked pretty relieved.'

'It makes sense for one of us to go,' Alison agreed, hoping she could hide the way her stomach had dropped.

She looked down at her eggs, and lost her appetite for them on the spot. So Nico was going to Cooma, while she was heading back to Corinbye? It had to happen. She'd known all along that it would happen. But would they even get a chance to say goodbye?

'How's Sarah?' she forced herself to ask.

'Very happy to be lowest priority on the casualty list,' Troy said. 'She's keeping her food and fluids down as long as she takes it carefully, and she can't wait to get home.'

'You're leaving the resort today?'

'We were scheduled to stay till Friday but, yes, we're bailing out.'

'I don't blame you. The smoke isn't going to clear for days, I imagine.'

'That has to be what's making her morning sickness so bad, not just all the drama. I want to get her home to Sydney, to some cleaner air. Just home, really.'

'Home… I think I've forgotten where it is.'

Troy laughed, but the words were truer than he could know.

'Enjoy those eggs,' he said. 'They've only got a few bits of ash in them.'

'I'll pretend it's pepper.'

He laughed again as he left, and Alison congratulated herself on her own performance. She forked some egg and toast into her mouth and it tasted like rubber. The coffee wasn't much better. Joan had settled down. Not so restless. Oxygen saturation improved. Heart graph more stable and normal. Alison stroked her pale, papery face and told her, 'You are incredible! I'm going to drink that champagne for you, if Troy can find it.'

Outside, Alison heard the sound of the chopper blades dying away, and two paramedics arrived with their boat-shaped red Stokes stretchers and equipment before she'd ploughed her way through a quarter of her breakfast.

They seemed like astronauts—visitors from another world—and their manner was typically upbeat and laced with black humour. 'You two gunning for our jobs or something?' one of them said to Nico and Alison, as they put blankets on the stretchers and set up oxygen and masks. 'Didn't have to have this lot in quite such organised shape, did you?'

'Yeah,' said the other. 'Could have taken pity on our

fragile egos and had the place in more chaos. Grateful sobbing at our arrival is always a nice touch, too.'

'Oh, trust me, we're grateful!' Alison drawled.

'How about we intubate our crico chappy a bit better, though? Ballpoint pen casings are not considered a good look in the emergency department.'

Their medical efficiency belied their way of talking. They administered high-flow oxygen, morphine for the burns. Kim's blood pressure had risen enough for a narcotic painkiller to be safe now, and they kept the dose low enough to guard against the drug's tendency to depress respiratory function.

Nico and Alison accompanied the crew on each trip out to the chopper, with Lefty, Joan and Kim. As the least seriously ill of the three, Kim went in a second army helicopter, mobilised due to the widespread nature of the bushfire emergency. With the strict safety protocols governing the landings and take-offs of such aircraft, those on the ground kept well back from the action, their hearts lifting in hope and relief as each helicopter rose in turn from the earth.

The ashen dust boiled in the wake of the downdraughts, and for a while the noise of the aircraft made speech impossible. Troy appeared out of nowhere with two glasses of champagne. 'Found it! Have some!'

Nico took a glass and raised it, his mood solemn and quiet. 'To safe arrivals and happy endings.' It felt more like a prayer than a toast.

'See you back at the house,' Troy said.

Alison and Nico stood for longer than they needed to, watching the army helicopter as it flew over the devastated terrain and out of sight, following the same flight path as the specialised med-evac chopper that had left several minutes earlier.

Finally, Nico told her, 'Jackie and Steve have a bag

packed and the baby ready. The firefighters are packed and ready, too.'

'You're going with them, Troy told me.'

He nodded. 'It seems like the best idea, don't you think?' He looked at her for a moment, and she caught the heat and the questions in the depths of his eyes before he looked away again.

'Yes,' she agreed. How could her throat have constricted so suddenly? 'The hospital's going to want to know what treatment we've given. Of course it makes sense. But…how will you get back to Corinbye? Hitch a ride on a fire truck?'

'I'm not going back. I can call the hotel from Cooma, fix up the bill and arrange to have my bags sent down. I may even make tonight's flight out of Sydney, but if I don't, I can make other plans. There'll be another flight twenty-four hours later.'

'Of course,' Alison answered, then added vaguely, 'Where are you flying to?'

It was a pointless question. Her mouth felt numb and uncomfortable, as if it was crammed with cotton wool.

'Rome.' He named the airline. 'Just for a few days, then on to London.'

'You must pick up a nice swag of frequent flyer miles.'

'Good for a free ticket every now and then,' he agreed.

'Right.'

Right. Say something, Alison. *Do* something!

Nico was watching her in silence, his incredible mint and coffee eyes warm yet full of so much doubt that she couldn't mistake it for anything else. The empty champagne glass dangled from one hand.

The day's heat was increasing by the minute, only marginally lessened by the pall of brown smoke keeping direct sunlight at bay, and yet her skin had gone clammy at the very thought that this was goodbye. His free hand closed around her forearm, and she wondered how it felt beneath his touch. Cold? Limp? She clutched him back, creating a kind of monkey grip. To her sizzling nerve-endings, his strong arm felt like a rope thrown to someone who was drowning.

'We want to say all sorts of things to each other, don't we?' he said in a low voice. She felt the brush of his forehead against her hair. 'But it's impossible.'

'Is it?' It didn't feel impossible right now, it felt vital, the only thing that could keep her breathing or walking in a straight line.

'You know it is.' His voice dropped still further, and the musical rhythm of his accent grew more marked. 'This isn't about the strength of what we feel in this moment. Of course we are going to feel strongly. We've all been halfway to hell and back in the past twenty-four hours. But I won't dishonour you, or myself, with some crazy, extravagant promise that won't seem real this time tomorrow. I won't risk telling you something that turns out to be a lie or an illusion. You're too important for that. You're worth so much more than that.'

And you're stronger than I am, Alison wanted to tell him. Because I'd say it all in a heartbeat, I'd take the risk, just for what it would give me now. I wouldn't think beyond this moment.

Which was his whole point, of course.

They had to think beyond this moment, and this place.

His grip tightened on her arm, and he seemed to have no words left. She couldn't look at him any more, so she stared down, absently noting the smear of ash across the pale front of his T-shirt and remembering how dewy and clean the skin beneath it had felt a few hours ago in the makeshift shower.

She felt his lips brush her forehead and temple, and the

warmth of his breath against her cheek, but she couldn't lift her face to meet the kiss the way he wanted. If she did, he would see the tears in her eyes. She blinked them back, waiting for him to take the hint and let her go.

He didn't, and her resolve weakened. How could she hold back from a kiss she wanted so much? She hooked cramped fingers over the waistband of his jeans, closed her eyes and tilted her head upwards. At once his mouth was there, meeting hers with such hunger and impatience that she could hardly breathe.

She held on to him, feeling that if she could just memorise this, memorise everything about it, even the acrid smell of the air, the blasting heat and the fatigue, then she might find the strength to see what had happened in the same way he did. She knew he had to be right, she just couldn't feel it, but maybe with this kiss…

Her whole body was heavy and melting by the time he pulled away.

'Please, tell me that you understand what I'm saying,' he said, his eyes searching her face.

'I do. How could I not? It's so—It's the only way to look at it.'

'OK, good. Well, that's something.'

They just kept looking at each other, waiting for a way to end this. Finally, he just shook his head and turned away. His shoulders were so square and stiff that she couldn't be in any doubt about how hard this was for him.

It helped.

Just a little.

'Say goodbye,' he growled, with his back to her. 'Say it, Alison. Please.'

'Goodbye,' she echoed obediently.

'Now go back to the house. And when the Fire Service vehicles have left, when you hear them go…'

He didn't finish the sentence. She didn't need him to. When the Fire Service vehicles had left, he would be gone and it would be safe for her to show her face again. Neither of them could stand to contemplate the risk and torment of a second goodbye.

As he'd asked, she walked back to the house, and did it without looking back to see if he was watching her. Inside, there was a fresh hum of activity and energy from the tour group as the awareness sank in that they would soon be leaving. The champagne had gone to their heads. Deirdre was still a little tearful.

'I don't know what to do,' she said. 'Joan and I have been friends for so long. I can't believe what's happened.'

'She has family, doesn't she?' Alison asked gently. 'Why don't you spend some time on the phone once we're back in Corinbye? You'll have details they won't have heard from the hospital, and there'll be practical help you can offer. Her children will be very grateful for that, and so will Joan herself once she's well again.'

Deirdre nodded, but still looked bewildered and sad. Alison patted her shoulder, then sought the solitude of the little bedroom which Jackie and Steve had fitted out for their baby in another lifetime, before the fire. She said goodbye to the new parents, who were happy to leave the farm and the animals in the safe hands of Frank and Rich.

About ten minutes later she heard the sound of the Fire Service vehicles moving down the track, then moved through the rest of the tour group's short time at the Porters' farm like a puppet, every smile and word and action mechanical and unreal. When she said goodbye to the remaining members of the Porter family, including the dogs, she felt as if she was leaving old friends.

The mini-bus arrived on schedule, its driver shocked by what he'd seen along the route. 'Unbelievable!'

With neither Joan nor Nico on board, there was one spare seat, which Valda fussed over, insisting that she and Jerry needed it between them. Her behaviour seemed to be bringing the group back full circle to their departure from the resort a little over twenty-four hours ago, but Alison knew that many if not most people would feel changed in real and important ways by the passage of the fire.

Seated beside Deirdre, she saw more tears rolling down the other woman's cheeks as the new driver ground his way slowly down the ash-covered farm track.

'Joan's in good hands now, Deirdre,' she said.

'I know. I just keep thinking how...' But she couldn't finish. For all of them, there was so much to say that silence was easiest. Eddie, Midori, Sarah, Troy... No one gave more than the odd, low-voiced murmur of disbelief.

They drove for more than twenty kilometres in a landscape utterly without colour. There was no wind today, and the smoke hung in the air like thick winter fog, shrouding the remnants of trees and mirroring the drab grey of the seared ground. The soil seemed as arid and lifeless as the moon, and if there were any birds or animals about, they were well hidden somewhere.

To the left, Alison saw a house that had been destroyed. She couldn't even tell what its walls had been made of, but its blackened iron roof lay on the ground like crumpled shreds of foil beside a burnt-out car. Later, she would learn that only three people in this entire region had lost their lives the previous day, and that the wildlife preserve they'd been due to visit on the tour had also been saved—miracles she would hardly have believed possible while on this journey.

Even when the mini-bus drove beyond the burnt area and into flatter and more thickly settled farmland, the greyness remained because of the smoke and the drought that had already stripped the paddocks of most of their vegetation. The first piece of irrigated lawn looked so green it was like a garish piece of nylon carpet. Somehow it almost hurt to look at it.

The mini-bus reached Corinbye at lunchtime. The fires had spared the resort village itself thus far, but there were still sections of the mountains that were burning out of control, and even though today's weather conditions offered some hope of getting parts of the blaze contained, a sense of potential danger remained strong. Emergency crews were converging on the area from as far away as Queensland and South Australia now.

Alison was booked on the two-o'clock shuttle to Cooma airport for a four-thirty flight to Byron Bay, via a change of plane in Sydney. As she packed, it occurred to her that Nico just might be on the same flight as far as Sydney. The possibility robbed her of her appetite for lunch, and she knew she was flirting with serious levels of exhaustion.

He wasn't on the plane.

For the best, really.

She sat back, did a crossword puzzle on the back page of the in-flight magazine and read a current affairs weekly, taking little of it in. At the luxurious Byron Bay resort, the tropical colour of sea and sky and vegetation hurt her eyes again, and when she opened her suitcase, she found that every item in it smelled of acrid smoke.

She despatched the lot down to the resort laundry, and raided the expensive boutique just behind the hotel, purchasing a casual outfit to wear until her clothing had come back clean. She showered thoroughly before putting it on, and remembered last night's shower with Nico in the shared intimacy of the canvas tent.

It had happened. It had been incredible. Yet her memory

of it seemed erratic, jumping from intensely relived sensation to total unreality in the space of a second.

She went for a sunset walk around the golf course adjacent to the resort and felt like a visitor from a distant planet. Fatigue soon dragged her back to her room, and she dropped into a sleep so deep that it only increased her sense of disorientation when she awoke the next morning.

'This is the first day of the rest of your life,' she told her reflection in the mirror, then laughed wryly.

She'd spent only a little over twenty-four hours with Nico. How could it have shattered her like this? No one else could possibly understand…except maybe Nico himself, and yet he'd still managed to say goodbye. He might be halfway to Europe by now.

Halfway to Rome.

The first day of the rest of her life.

The fire.

Strength.

Change.

Suddenly, she knew what she had to do, and she knew that she had the courage she needed. She *had* to have it, because this was too important for safe habits and comfort zones to count.

There was no one waiting in line at the first and business class check-in desk at Nico's chosen airline on Monday evening. There was never anyone waiting at their first and business class check-in, which was one of the reasons he usually flew with them. Tonight, for the first time in his life, he regretted the lack of waiting.

No more excuses to stall, after he'd successfully done so for more than twenty-four hours. He could have been on his scheduled evening flight out of Australia this time yesterday because he could have been on the four-thirty flight from

Cooma to Sydney. Instead, he'd stalled at the hospital, making sure the fire casualties were scheduled for appropriate treatment, talking to more staff than he needed to, delaying the phone call to the resort hotel in Corinbye that would trigger the despatch of his luggage.

He'd strolled into the town's main street and found a wood-fired pizza restaurant for a late lunch, and had lingered over the meal until he'd started getting odd looks from the waitress. He'd even drunk a glass of wine. He'd arrived at the airport to find his luggage safely awaiting him, but his flight already taxiing along the runway with its propellers whirling, and he hadn't been sorry to see it go.

There weren't any more seats that evening, although a helpful member of the airline ground staff told him he might be able to charter something if it was urgent.

Nico decided it wasn't, and spent the night in a motel, including an hour in the rather dingy motel laundry room, machine-washing the smoke out of his clothes, since the motel didn't run the kind of housekeeping service that whisked it away for you and brought it back ironed and folded.

Sitting alone beneath the fluorescent lights with the tumble dryer banging noisily in the background, he idly tried to pinpoint when he'd last washed his own clothes…when his clothes had ever needed washing as much as they did today…but instead found himself thinking of one of the things he and Alison had talked about during their night-time walk—the way she never used to take care of herself properly and never used to delegate sufficiently to others either.

He smiled, and then his stomach dropped.

Now, watching the desk clerk look up from her computer terminal and prepare to greet him, his stomach dropped again, and instead of reaching for his passport he told her, 'I'd like to reschedule my flight.'

For the second time in as many days.

'Certainly sir. You'll be staying here in Sydney?'

'No, I'm going to head north for a few days.'

'So you'll reschedule for…?'

'Let's try Friday,' he said.

'Friday. Let's see, shall we?' The computer keys began to rattle beneath her fingers.

The long row of airport check-in desks appeared in Alison's vision across a crowd of departing travellers, and there he was, standing in front of it.

Nico.

The Conti Pharmaceuticals heir, about to take his flight home. He wore casual trousers in a light khaki beige, with a plain black T-shirt on top, he had a pair of expensive sunglasses pushed high on his head, and his classic profile was unmistakable.

She hadn't known if he'd be here, or if he would be twenty-four hours ahead of her, and she'd thought that it didn't matter, but now she knew it did. Was she really ready for this? Brave enough? Oh, she was. She had to be.

He hadn't seen her yet.

His gaze canvassed the crowded departure terminal, arrowed towards the shops and eating places visible beyond the check-in desks, skated past the luggage trolleys lined up just inside the entrance, and then fell on Alison as she came towards him.

He looked shocked.

And then he smiled—the smile that lit up his whole face, made her feel as if she was walking on air, and always seemed meant just for her. She knew it so well, but every time she saw it, it cast the same magic spell in her heart. She'd been so scared that she wouldn't see it this time—

that he'd frown and shake his head, and something would die forever inside her.

But, no, he'd smiled.

They met in front of the check-in desk, and she felt as if this spot was the only fixed place in her universe, while everything else circled dizzily around them.

'You got here just in time,' he said.

She nodded. 'You're about to go through to the gate. I'm on the same flight. First class. It was all they had left.'

'What?'

She lifted her chin. 'I called the airline this morning and managed to book myself on the same flight, cancelled the rest of my stay in Byron Bay and flew down this afternoon. I'm not going to accept what you said to me yesterday morning, Nico. I'm just not. I want to give this whole thing more of a chance. I don't care if it's crazy, I—'

He wasn't even looking at her. He'd turned back to the desk. 'Look, excuse me, can I cancel what I just asked, or have you already keyed it in?' he said to the check-in clerk.

Her fingers paused over the keys. 'You want to fly today after all?'

'Nico?'

'Yes, please.'

'You got me just in time,' the clerk said. 'Your seat for today's flight is still available. Are you checking in now?'

'Um…' He looked at Alison. 'I don't think so. And I think there's a chance we may want to change our seating assignment…' He dropped his voice. 'Change our whole future, Alison? Let's not hold up these next people…'

'No, OK,' she just managed to say as they moved aside.

'Is it? OK, I mean? That I was about to reschedule my flight for Friday and rush up to Byron Bay to tell you I didn't want to let this go?'

'That's what you and the check-in clerk were talking about?'

'Yes.'

'Is it *OK*, Nico?' She laughed. 'It was my idea first, wasn't it? It's better than OK, it's, oh, it's…' Her voice was not quite steady. 'Can't you tell just *how* OK it is?' She couldn't begin to summon any pretence about it, and just grinned helplessly as tears began to blur in her eyes.

'Well, you see, this isn't what we agreed was sensible yesterday,' he said, with a hesitancy that tore at Alison's heart. He was playing her usual role, and she was playing his.

She took a breath and searched his face, inches away from him now. 'Let's get this straight. You're not interested in being sensible any more, right?'

He shook his head. 'I tried to be sensible. I have spent a long and very sleepless twenty-four hours trying as hard as I could to be the absolute archetype of good sense. It didn't work. Now, in sheer desperation, Alison, I am prepared to consider other alternatives…' He grasped her hands. 'You're cold?'

'Just my hands. Just since I saw you standing here.' She tried to laugh. 'That can be the effect of sheer desperation, I've found. Nico, just yesterday you told me that the only possible thing was to say goodbye, that you wouldn't make promises that would turn out to be lies or delusions. And I—I *bought* all of that utterly then because it was the only thing that made sense. This morning, I rebelled and decided to follow you to Rome to tell you how I felt, to take my courage in my hands and ask if we could take the really crazy first step together. I hadn't expected to find that you'd already made the same journey.'

'I would have questioned my own judgement and my priorities for the rest of my life if I'd simply let it go. We

saw fate and chance and miracles when the fire came
through on Saturday evening, but I was too shattered to
understand what those things were saying to us. But I've
had enough time to think about it now. It was easy, as it
turned out. We have to find out whether fate has another
miracle in store for us, don't we? There's just no other
choice.'

He wrapped his arms around her and pulled her close
against his chest. She pillowed her head there, speechless
with happiness and hope, almost unable to believe that this
was real. He began to kiss her, and she put her whole soul
into her response, feeling the tears still wet and sticky on
her lashes.

'So how long do we have?' she managed at last. She
could almost hear the clock ticking in her mind. 'I'm due
back at work next Wednesday.'

'We have the flight together. We have five days in Rome.
I fly to London on Sunday. Fly with me, and then across to
Chicago on Tuesday. Don't you think that might be long
enough?'

'Yes, more than long enough.'

'After that, we'll do what it takes. We'll meet whenever
we can. In Europe, in Chicago. Halfway across the Atlantic
Ocean, for all I care. And we'll find a way to create what
we want. I hope and know with all my heart that it will be
a future we can share.'

'Oh, Nico, so do I, so do I!'

He kissed her again, laughed at her tears, pulled a paper
tissue from his pocket and wiped them away. 'Let me guess,
you don't have one of these?'

'Um, no.'

'What am I going to do with you?'

'Marry me, maybe?'

'I think it's the only answer.'

EPILOGUE

NICO married his beautiful bride in Italy in March, with the first hints of spring filling the air. They had the best reasons in the world for not wanting to wait longer.

'We've wasted so much time already,' Nico told Alison the day in late January when he formally proposed over dinner high above Chicago in a restaurant at the top of one of the city's tallest buildings. 'Let's not waste any more, for my father's sake.'

Everyone knew that Antonio Conti did not have much time left. He was in the process of relinquishing personal control of the family corporation to a new board headed by his nephew Massimo. Nico would sit on the board, but would not continue his role in the day-to-day running of the corporation. He and his father had had a long and very honest conversation at Christmas over the question of his future.

'If you really want to practise medicine, Niccolo, then that is what you should do,' Antonio had said. 'We don't often get a second chance in this life. I was given one after my first surgery, and I did not take it seriously, as I should have done. I don't want you to make the same mistake. Not with Alison, and not with your future.'

'I'd like to practise in America, Dad. I want to study paediatrics there. Alison's career would be much harder to move.'

'Of course, and we are so proud of her success. Will you let me be sentimental about it, since we all know that now is not the time to hold back?'

'Yes, Dad, say whatever you want,' Nico had urged him.

'She has blossomed so much. She has swept away all the doubts we had before, my son. Of course you and she must decide together what is best for both of you.'

'She's started learning Italian, but that's a long way from being able to practise here in Italy.' Nico had chosen not to mention, too, that Alison's vocabulary so far had a strong lean towards such distinctly non-medical expressions as 'I love you', 'Kiss me again' and 'You have beautiful eyes'.

'Your mother likes to travel,' his father had said. 'She will fly to America several times a year for shopping expeditions...and babysitting,' he'd added slyly.

Although neither man had known it at the time, Faustina Conti's skill with babies would be called upon sooner than planned—which was another good reason not to delay the wedding. Their baby was due at the end of September, and the figure-hugging ivory satin gown that Alison had chosen did not lend itself to last-minute letting out at the seams.

So far, the pregnancy was proving easy for her. Her hair had grown extra thick and lustrous, and her skin glowed. Nico barely saw the ornate decorations in the church, barely heard the words he spoke, barely tasted the food served in the elegant private banquet room at one of Rome's best restaurants. All he could focus on was his new bride.

'Hasn't this been a perfect day, everything just the way we wanted?' Alison whispered to him as his hand closed over hers and they cut the wedding cake together, late in the evening.

'Ask me a month from now, when we've come back from our honeymoon and seen the photos,' he whispered back. 'Because I'm in such a daze, I haven't taken anything in except you.'

'I think we'll be happy with the photos,' she predicted. And, after two lazy, sunny weeks in the Caribbean, they were.

Copies were made of the best one, showing Nico and Alison, Antonio and Faustina, and Doretta and a handsome Conti second cousin in his mid-fifties, who had been assigned as Alison's mother's escort for the day and hadn't seemed to object to the job at all.

And several copies went from Chicago halfway across the globe to Jackie and Steve, to Deirdre and Joan and to the Corinbye District Rural Fire Service, around whose headquarters green grass had begun to grow after good autumn rain.

MILLS & BOON®

Live the emotion

0505/03b

_MedicaL
romance™

THE HEART SURGEON'S PROPOSAL

by Meredith Webber   (Jimmie's Children's Unit)

Paediatric anaesthetist Maggie Walsh fell in love with surgery fellow Phil Park when they both joined the elite Children's Cardiac Unit. But he never seemed to look her way – until the night they fell into bed! Now Maggie is pregnant! Phil will do the right thing – for the baby's sake – but Maggie won't consent to a loveless marriage…

EMERGENCY AT THE ROYAL *by Joanna Neil*

Dr Katie Sherbourn knows she shouldn't get too close to A&E consultant Drew Bradley. It would upset her ill father and alienate her from her beloved family. But memories of her relationship with Drew leave Katie yearning for his touch. And working closely with him at the Royal forces her to confront her feelings…

THE MEDICINE MAN *by Dianne Drake*   (24/7)

Chayton Ducheneaux turned his back on his Sioux roots for life as a high-powered Chicago surgeon. He'd never give it up to return home. But then he meets the reservation doctor, Joanna Killian. She's dedicated, determined – and beautiful. And as the attraction between them grows Chay learns what being a doctor – and a man – is really about…

On sale 3rd June 2005

Available at most branches of WHSmith, Tesco, ASDA, Martins, Borders, Eason, Sainsbury's and all good paperback bookshops.

Visit www.millsandboon.co.uk

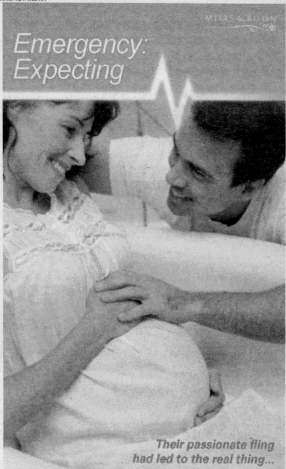

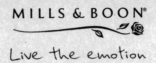

FREE

4 BOOKS AND A SURPRISE GIFT!

We would like to take this opportunity to thank you for reading this Mills & Boon® book by offering you the chance to take FOUR more specially selected titles from the Medical Romance™ series absolutely FREE! We're also making this offer to introduce you to the benefits of the Reader Service™—

- ★ **FREE home delivery**
- ★ **FREE gifts and competitions**
- ★ **FREE monthly Newsletter**
- ★ **Books available before they're in the shops**
- ★ **Exclusive Reader Service offers**

Accepting these FREE books and gift places you under no obligation to buy; you may cancel at any time, even after receiving your free shipment. Simply complete your details below and return the entire page to the address below. You don't even need a stamp!

YES! Please send me 4 free Medical Romance books and a surprise gift. I understand that unless you hear from me, I will receive 6 superb new titles every month for just £2.75 each, postage and packing free. I am under no obligation to purchase any books and may cancel my subscription at any time. The free books and gift will be mine to keep in any case.

M5ZEE

Ms/Mrs/Miss/Mr..Initials ....
                                                      BLOCK CAPITALS PLEASE

Surname ....

Address ....

....

....Postcode ....

Send this whole page to:
The Reader Service, FREEPOST CN81, Croydon, CR9 3WZ